Abe And Ellie

An Unlikely Couple

C. J. Maloney

ISBN: 9798841256137

CONTENTS

ACKNOWLEDGMENTS

My family provides me with joy, support, and a model for what tribal life should look like. There are not words enough to thank my wife.

1 THE INCIDENT

Ellie

It wasn't that Ellie didn't expect to be attacked. Frees always expected to be attacked. But it wasn't likely as long as the grey sky still faintly outlined the jagged posts of the border wall like uneven, rotting teeth. Ellie still scanned through her sight's infrared crosshairs at a break in the wall filled in by fat rusting coils of barbed wire and the reddish vines of the Wilds pushing through.

Twenty paces away, surrounded by a steam cloud, Fat Abe kept fiddling with his doodads at the thermal tower. His dark round head bobbed over his mottled overalls as he clucked over the damage. Ellie puffed a small steam cloud of her own in irritation and pulled her guard's jacket closer around her. Now that the sun wasn't beating down on the sha sector the temperature was dropping. But Ellie had worn her spring guard's jacket because Todd said it looked good on her. Now she was getting stiff with the cold. She flexed her fingers and thought about Mama's warm coffee in the mess hall. But she had to protect the stupid 'Cycler until he was done.

If she'd had any choice, Ellie would have skipped guarding Fat Abe, the most annoying 'Cycler she knew. He always knew everything about everything. In border school when his hand went up, she and all the other Free cadets would groan. When they'd been growing up, her mother had forced them to play together because she was friends with Abe's mom. Dumb little fat Abe had shown Ellie his secret pet, one of those nasty mutated chipmunks from the other side of the wall. Of course, Ellie had turned him over to Papa, as any Free daughter should. She and Abe hadn't really spoken since.

Ellie rolled her shoulders in her black guard's tunic, repositioned her braid by shaking her head, and glanced back at the twinkling lights of the two-milers looming in the distance behind her beyond the empty alienation zone. Even guarding Fat Abe was better than being stuck inside one of those giant pyramids, trapped in the small spaces where she couldn't breathe or run. But even thinking that made Ellie feel guilty. She knew her place was inside with Mama. It really wasn't a Free woman's place to be on the line.

If Papa had any choice, Ellie would be stuck helping Mama in the sha sector pantry. But Ellie knew the sha sector border wall security was already too thin. Papa complained about it constantly to the big shots at Central. World city Bela behind them was full of people, stuffed into those two-mile high skyscrapers like so many bullets in an ammo clip. But none of those employees wanted to do real work like police the border wall. Ellie had heard they'd even rather go mine on the asteroid belt than protect the radioactive border. So the Frees like Ellie's family, descended from the last holdouts of the Corporate Wars, were all that was left. Dubsee Central was supposed to supply them with enough recruits, but that had never happened in Papa's lifetime.

As contractors, Frees didn't have the same rights as employees. They didn't have anyone who would argue their case for them at Central. So, in desperation, the Frees had finally broken with tradition and started promoting their own older boys to help run the line. When that wasn't enough, even their womenfolk got called up to fill the gaps in rotation duty. Papa's loss was Ellie's gain. Ellie was outside in the air rather than in some backroom making bread. She stared down along the tangled border wall line and swung up her rifle for another scan.

As she scanned, Ellie daydreamed she was on this babysitting guard duty with her boyfriend, Todd. He was working twenty clicks down the line in the che sector, trying to make a name for himself. She missed Todd. But she respected him for volunteering for the line before he reached recruitment age. Todd was everything a man should be, and Ellie knew they'd be together when the time was right. He'd even hinted that he'd already put a downpayment on their wedding weapons. Todd would get promoted. When he earned enough credits Ellie could move to stay at the che barracks and care for their children. Well, their child, because they were limited to just one like everyone in World City. But according to Ellie's mom Gladys, just having one had been more than a full-time job. Ellie believed her because were still numerous holes in their barrack quarters where Ellie had run into the walls.

Fat Abe had dropped something and was rooting around for it in the darkness. Ellie wondered what would happen if she just walked off and left him for the Arcwolves. Maybe she could say he sent her on an errand. She momentarily imagined him being ravaged and smiled to herself. It would serve his mutie-loving butt right. But then she thought of what Papa would do. He would never consider leaving his post regardless of his feelings about the 'Cyclers. She squared her shoulders and scanned the Border fence again.

The Skullrons, those nasty mutant chipmunks Abe loved, were feeling frisky tonight. They were chasing each other along the border wall, in and out of the pitted barbed wire. The Arcwolves could be hunting along the other side. If the Skullrons breached the wall, the Arcwolves might breach as well. The border wall was a junk pile of old rusty barbed wire and ancient corroded posts, with new layers of wire thrown over the top of it like a fresh coat of paint on a rotting hovercar. They'd needed a new border wall for as long as anyone could remember. But every year it seemed to slip off the budget of the Energy Production Division.

That's all the border zone was to Dubsee. Energy production. It meant that the Frees were just the contracted security detail for the 'Cyclers. The 'Cyclers were more important to Dubsee. They were true employees, while the Frees were just Grunts leftover from the losing side of the Corporate Wars, disposable labor. 'Cyclers managed the thermal plants along the border that pumped endless amounts of hissing steam into the generator turbines. If it got cold enough, the steam would be sent straight through great underground tunnels to heat the two-miler skyscrapers. Otherwise the steam was turned into power by the 'Cyclers. All the Frees did was guard the 'Cyclers' backs.

Ellie did another sweep, then squared her shoulders against the cold like a good Free should. Abe had better fix whatever doodad had gone wrong with the thermal tower thingie. It was taking him long enough!

As contractors, Frees got no respect, no promotions, and no credit raises. It had gotten so bad some of the Frees joked about walking off the job. Let the Arcwolves wander into World City Bella. Then Dubsee would realize just how important the Frees were, much more important than the 'Cyclers. But when the Arcwolves had gotten through before the Frees lost their jobs and their leaders got shipped out to the asteroid belt.

According to Papa that breach hadn't even been the Frees' fault. They'd been hunting out in the Wilds trying to exterminate the Arcwolves. The Arcwolves had circled behind them, jumped the border wall, and run wild in the city. Most of them had left back to the Wilds, but every now and then the news would report an Arcwolf sighting. The news teams would replay the old footage of shadowy packs roaming the streets, repeating over and over the lie about the failure of the Frees to protect the city. Papa would turn off the news and need to go out to the firing range every time. Not that those stories gave the Frees any new recruits or a new wall. They were stuck. But no matter how bad it got, Papa was right. The Frees would never abandon their duty.

However good her jacket looked, Ellie was starting to shiver. She wanted to ask if Fat Abe was almost done, but it would break her long silence with him. He was the one who'd been breaking the rules all those years ago by having a Skullron pet. She'd done the right thing by reporting him. If Abe wanted to hold a grudge by giving her the silent treatment, that was his problem.

On Ellie's right, she saw a flash out of the corner of her eye. It sure looked like an Arcwolf flash, the little sparks they gave off when they got angry. Ellie swung the rifle sight around and scanned. Nothing. But… no, nothing. Then she heard the growl.

Ellie swung her rifle back. Caught in the infrared, Fat Abe was backing up slowly. He was between her and whatever he was backing from. Ellie wanted to yell at him to move but bit her tongue. One, she wasn't going to break their silence first. Two, any loud noise could send the Arcwolf into a frenzy.

But Fat Abe was smart. Through the roof smart. So surely he must know where she was and get out of the way to give her the shot?

Ellie watched as Fat Abe got down on his hands and knees. He rolled onto his back, with his belly exposed and his arms and legs in the air. Was he trying to give the Arcwolf the easiest target to his fat belly?

But beyond Fat Abe, Ellie could now see the Arcwolf. It was spitting sparks, faint in the blackness. So it wasn't really mad yet. Along the lower edge of its throat, Ellie could see a long, deep jagged cut. Just like an arrow pointing to its heart. This wasn't just any Arcwolf, this was Scar. Scar was the Arcwolf Papa said had killed Granpa. Babysitting had just paid off. Ellie could already see Papa's satisfied smile when he got to give old Scar's dead body a well-deserved kick. Maybe even a word of praise for his sharp-shooting girl.

Ellie breathed in, sighted high along her rifle by about an inch on Scar's chest since her Springfield shot a bit low, and breathed out as she gently pressed the trigger straight back. The Arcwolf jumped at the same moment she felt the recoil in her shoulder and heard the shot bounce back from the Border fence. A good, clean shot. Fat Abe owed her his life. The Arcwolf was down.

But instead of lying flat as it should have, the Arcwolf was getting back to its feet. It didn't even look unsteady. But it was sparking like crazy, so it was mad. No matter, Ellie had time for a second shot. She had already jacked a new bullet into the chamber without thinking faster than the smoking shell could fall to the ground. Let's see how well it moved after a headshot. Not as sure a target, but…Ellie looked through her sight. The Arcwolf was gone.

Ellie felt panic. She couldn't panic, Frees didn't panic. She scanned left and right, but nothing picked up on the infrared. So she reached up and pulled her field back, making it wider. Wide enough to see the lumbering shape of Fat Abe bearing down on her from the left. Then he was on top of her, pushing her down. Her rifle flipped up and she heard her sight smash as it hit the broken pavement above her.

"Stay down," said Fat Abe. "Don't move. Maybe I can still fix this…"

Ellie heard the growl coming from behind her. She tried to twist around, but Abe's weight held her down. Ellie wanted to punch Abe in the throat, send him hacking and coughing to the ground. But he was crooning, making a noise almost like a baby dog. It didn't sound like it was working. The growl was getting louder, and under Abe's arm, Ellie could see the sparks coming off the Arcwolf.

Then Ellie heard a whistle. Three long, one short. The Arcwolf stopped growling, but Ellie could see it was still there. The whistle repeated, and the Arcwolf was gone.

Fat Abe breathed a sigh of relief. A drop of his stinging sweat dripped down into Ellie's eye. She reached up to wipe it away and realized she couldn't with Abe lying flat on top of her.

"Get off! Get off!" Ellie shoved at Fat Abe.

"I'm going...I'm stuck," Fat Abe twisted. "I think one of my hex key wrenches is hooked into your belt."

"So unhook it."

"What do you think I'm doing?"

"I think you're fiddling around with my pants."

"It's easier to undo your belt."

"Well, hurry up." Ellie could feel herself start to hyperventilate under his weight. She was remembering, feeling trapped in that locked cupboard from years ago. Ellie was in the dark, alone, and she couldn't get out. She forced herself to stay calm, to breather slower.

"Is it done?"

"No, I think the wrench is stuck in the loop. Hang on, I'll try to jiggle it loose." Fat Abe moved his hips around.

Ellie heard running boots coming fast. "Get off!" She shoved hard at Fat Abe. Something tore in her pants.

"What's going on here?" A voice boomed out of the darkness. Ellie dropped her hands. Great, just great. It was Papa.

2 LOST

Ilya

Ilya Patton had been raised on the line. He'd lost his father and grandfather in the last hunting party that never returned. Everything he did was for the safety of a huge, anonymous, and uncaring Dubsee city that loomed in the distance like some sullen, forgotten God. Ilya was responsible for the safety of a bunch of stuck-up 'Cycler thermal jockeys who never shaved and wore garbage rather than uniforms. So when Ilya saw his daughter Ellie under one of those thermal jockeys, lying on the ground under some fat kid's writhing, sweating belly when she was supposed to be on guard duty, of course, he was furious.

"Get off her!" Ilya swung the back of his rifle into the side of Fat Abe's head. The kid went down without a sound.

Ellie scrambled to her feet. "You didn't have to do that, Papa. He was just getting off."

Ilya paused his rifle butt, breathed out a cloud of steam in the cold air, and stared at his daughter. "He wasn't forcing himself on you?"

"No! Nothing was happening, Papa. Really. There was an Arcwolf. I shot it."

Ilya looked around at the surrounding ground. "If you shot it, where is it?"

"It got up."

Ilya laughed in disbelief. "You missed? My daughter missed? You haven't missed anything since you were twelve."

Ellie flushed with shame. "No, I hit it. Straight shot to the heart. But it shook it off and got back up."

Ilya snorted. "Impossible. So you did miss and it got away. Maybe you missed it because you were distracted by your little 'Cycler boyfriend here. Is that the story you're telling me?"

"No." Ellie stood her ground. "I hit it straight on. It just got up and attacked me."

"OK," Ilya slid his rifle strap back over his shoulder and crossed his arms. "So why aren't you dead?"

"Fat Abe protected me."

"He protected you? This fat 'Cycler boy protected you? How? By lying on you and grinding his hips?" Ilya was getting redder in the face. "Listen. Maybe what you want to tell me is that your rifle went off when it hit the rocks. You broke it because you were fooling around. That's what really happened, da?"

"No!" Ellie was losing her own temper. "He was trying to protect me."

"How? He has no weapon. Was he using a wrench? Those little doohickies on his belt? How was he protecting you?"

Ellie finally looked like she was starting to realize how crazy she sounded. "He was protecting me by...singing something."

Ilya laughed. "You want me to believe that Fat Abe scared away a disappearing Arcwolf by singing to it? That's a pretty scary voice he's got."

Papa wasn't joking around. He didn't believe her and now he was trying to decide what to do about her failure of duty. Here on the line, the sector leader was judge and jury. If he decided she was a failure he would have to report her to Central. Central could terminate her contract. She could be cast out, made into a Wanderer, and shipped off to the asteroid mines.

Ellie hurried on. "The singing didn't work, Papa. But somebody called the Arcwolf. Whistled for it from the other side of the wall. So it left."

"Wait, now you're telling me this was a tame Arcwolf? Some Wanderer is training Arcwolves now? Magical Arcwolves who don't die and who hate 'Cycler singing?" Ilya rocked back on his heels and shook his head. "That's a crazy story, my dornoy daughter. You should have stuck with shooting at an Arcwolf and missing. Or maybe just been honest with me from the first. Admit you like messing around with Fat Abe on duty. I knew it was a bad idea to put women on the line. Too easily distracted."

"No, Papa. I wasn't messing around."

Ilya could feel his face getting red. "Don't insult me! I wasn't born yesterday! Look at your pants!" Ellie looked down. Her belt was hanging loose. A patch of pale skin and her lower hair was clearly visible. "Fix yourself." Ilya turned away from her. His jaw worked while Ellie pulled up her pants and redid her belt. "I'm ashamed of you. If you're going to mess around, destroy your virtue, at least do it off duty! I didn't raise my daughter to be a...slusha...and with one of these 'Cycler animals? What about Todd? Have you no honor?" Ilya was working himself into one of his blind rages, the ones he'd promised he was done with once he married Mama.

Ellie muttered as she tucked in her belt and straightened her black tunic, covering herself. "Nothing happened."

Ilya could hear her. He turned in a fury with his fist clenched. At the last moment, he stopped himself, but his open hand still caught Ellie lightly on the cheek with a smack. "Nahui! You lie to my face! And because of your lie, your imaginary Arcwolf sighting, I have to report a wall breach and turn you over to Central! Do you know what that means? Did you think of what your lie will do to your Mama? You can be cast out, made a wanderer. It means they could take you and put you on a ship to the 'belt. How could you do this to me, to your Mama?" He turned away so Ellie couldn't see his tears. "Now clean up your 'Cycler garbage. You are confined to barracks. I've got to get back to work. Some of us have got a line to guard."

Ellie

Ilya turned his back on Ellie and stalked away. Only when his boots had faded did Ellie allow a single tear to trickle down her cheek. Her cheek stung a bit, but her pride ached. She'd been the best marksman in Papa's class. Her obstacle course time had rivaled even Todd's record. For Ellie's whole life she'd proved to Papa over and over again that she was a better son for him than any boy he could have had. But Papa never saw her that way. He was always just one step away from calling her a stupid girl and telling her to get back in the kitchen with Mama. Now this idiot 'Cycler had broken her perfect streak, given Papa a reason to take away her rifle and send her back to the pantry for good. A life spent in small, dark rooms. Ellie felt suffocation well up in her chest.

"Wow, he sure was mad." Fat Abe rolled over on the ground.

Ellie looked down at him in disgust. "You were awake? The whole time?" She didn't even mention that they hadn't talked in years and she preferred it that way.

"Well, most of it," Fat Abe pushed himself up slowly. "He got me good, but I've got a thick head. I figured it was better to play dead. Didn't sound like he was in a listening mood. I've had a lot of experience with bullies."

"Papa is not a bully!" Ellie automatically defended him.

"Says the girl with the red cheek," said Fat Abe. "Can I get a hand up?" He reached out to Ellie for a hand. She turned her back on him.

"Whatever." Fat Abe groaned as he climbed to his feet. "Good thing I just finished the coupling when that Arcwolf jumped the fence. We can go in now."

"So you saw it?" Ellie couldn't help herself. The whole episode seemed like a crazy dream that she'd made up in her head. Papa's version of things made so much more sense. But if Fat Abe had seen it too, then it hadn't been a dream.

"Yeah, 'course I saw it. And I think I could have gotten it to go away except you decided to shoot it. I've been learning about Arcwolf pack behavior for years. My mom's an expert."

"If I hadn't shot it, you'd be dead." Ellie was certain. "The only thing you were doing was giving it a tour of your juicy bits before it feasted on you."

"No," Fat Abe switched to that condescending tone that he got when he knew better. "I was showing it submissive behavior. It's classic nonviolence. But I guess a dumb shoot-first-never-ask-questions Free would be the last person to understand that."

"This dumb Free was the only thing between you and being Arcwolf chow," Ellie retorted. "So let's get going, Fatso."

Fat Abe looked at her in the faint glow of the lamps and used his superior voice. "Your dad just relieved you of duty. So I'll make my own fat way back, thanks."

Ellie fought the urge to hit him with her rifle butt. Her beautiful rifle, which now lay with its sight bent and a scattering of glass where the impact had broken one of her magnifying lenses. Instead, she ignored Fat Abe and bent down to see the damage. She could hear Fat Abe clanking away into the darkness, all the little tools on his work belt bumping into each other like he was a damn wind chime. No self-respecting Free would have a belt like that, because it broadcast your location to any mutation within a hundred mets. But then, the 'Cyclers probably wanted to attract the mutations. Especially Fat Abe, with his dumb cute little baby Skullron.

Standing up with her broken rifle, Ellie yelled after Fat Abe, "Mutie lover!"

3 MUTIE LOVER

Abe

"Mutie lover!"

Abe felt the insult as much as heard it. He wondered why it still hurt so much after all these years. Maybe it was because he'd trusted Ellie once, thought she could keep his secret.

A noise off to Abe's left made him jump. It was just a Skullron, running in and out of the barbed wire. Smiling, Abe wondered if it was related to Cyrano.

Abe had found Cyrano, a little abandoned Skullron, along the edge of the border wall. Cyrano had barely been mutated, just the start of an extra pair of legs coming off his hindquarters. Abe thought they looked like little spare legs that would grow if Cyrano ever lost a leg to an Arcwolf.

It wasn't like Abe had wanted to keep Cyrano. Cyrano had followed him. Yeah, probably it was because Abe always had something to eat in his coverall pockets. But the little Skullron had darted along and peered up at Abe from every crevice, its huge eyes peeking from that tiny skull-like face until Abe had laughed and tossed the little Skullron a piece of his sandwich. He knew it was against the rules, but he figured Cyrano had earned it.

The next day, Cyrano had been there again. Abe wasn't sure where the Skullron hid during the night, but with Abe, he got bolder and bolder. Pretty soon Cyrano was running right alongside Abe like a trained puppy. Abe got him to beg, to stay, to fetch, and to come and go on command, which was pretty good for a Skullron.

Then they had a really cold night, the coldest Abe could remember. Abe couldn't sleep well thinking about Cyrano out there shivering. So the next day he'd taken some rags from the 'Cycler recycling piles and built a little nest for Cyrano under the thermal pipes where it was warm and Cyrano would be out of the rain. Even though he was a Skullron, a bad rain could still burn Cyrano's skin - especially if it came up out of the radioactive Wilds from the south.

It was about that time that Abe decided to call him Cyrano, mostly because of the Skullron's almost non-existent nose. The lack of nose made Abe think of an ancient Beforer vid of a man with a long nose named Cyrano. So Abe thought it was funny to call this little no-nose creature Cyrano, just to remind Cyrano of what he lacked.

Abe stopped and looked up at the 'Cycler barracks festooned with bits of colored cloth and makeshift energy devices. It contrasted with the Free barracks that were drab except for their silent gun towers. Abe wiped his nose before starting the stair climb up to the third floor sha sector quarters he shared with his family. His first stop was the workshop, but hopefully, dad wouldn't be there to quiz him about his first solo repair. The stairs looked steeper in the dim, flickering light. Maybe he really was finally getting fat.

In the first year of border school, Ilya had come into the newly formed school for both Free cadets and 'Cycler children to take all the kids' measurements for uniforms. All the girls got their measurements taken with their shirts on, but all the boys took their shirts off. Abe had taken his 'Cycler rag-cloth shirt off and sucked in his stomach to try and impress everyone. He didn't realize how much skinnier he was than the muscular Free kids. When he sucked in his stomach, Abe looked like he was starving. So an older Free kid named Todd had looked over at Abe and whistled. "You sure are fat, Abe." Everyone laughed.

Fat Abe. The name stuck. Even when Abe got bigger and worked hard at building muscle. Lately, he'd started to put on some belly fat, just like his dad. It wasn't a choice, it was genetics. But try telling the other kids that. So Abe had really become Fat Abe to fit his nickname. He guessed "slightly overweight Abe" didn't quite have the same ring.

Abe slapped open the workshop door. Once it might have been tidy, but his dad worked all hours on his projects these days, leaving them in hunched piles like broken creatures on the workbenches. Abe cleared himself a space for his toolbelt and took it off with a heave. He'd lost his three-sixteenths hex key wrench, so he flicked on his flashlight to root around for a new one in the old bin of spares.

It was bad enough to be Fat Abe. But when Cyrano got found because Ellie told on him, he became Fat Abe the mutie lover. Abe should have never trusted Ellie with Cyrano's hiding place. He'd been trying to impress her, trying to make her like him, and it had backfired.

Ellie had always been the golden girl. Commander Ilya's only child. She was faster, stronger, and ruthless in any competition. With her angular face, rippling muscles, and long dirty blonde braid, Abe had to admit she was really attractive in that, "Break your arm for you" macho Free girl way. Of course he had a crush on her, every boy at border school did. She'd been paying attention to him that day. It was like having an Arcwolf in your room, exciting and scary at the same time. Sure, it had only been because their mothers wanted to really talk and sent them off together. Ellie had beaten Abe at every physical game, and she didn't want to play the card or board games that he won against everyone. She'd seemed so impressed when Abe told her he had a secret. It had been so exciting to bring her down into the thermal pipes, seeing her face flush with anticipation. Only when he'd showed her Cyrano, Abe had that sinking feeling in his gut that he'd made a mistake.

Ellie hadn't wanted to touch the Skullron and asked if it was radioactive. Abe had assured her that it was as safe as background radiation. But Ellie had looked away and said it was time to get back. She'd outrun him back to the barracks. When Abe got there his mother and Ellie's mother were arguing. They just stopped when he came in. Ellie and her mother left without saying goodbye.

The next day, Ilya came to their quarters and ordered Abe to show him Cyrano's nest. Abe had cried, but even his mother told him they couldn't have Skullrons on this side of the border wall. His dad Franklin told him that the Skullrons could end up nesting in all the thermals' electrical systems and disrupt power. It just wasn't a reasonable choice, not relevant to the tasks at hand.

Abe had hated his dad right then, with his dark face set in a smirk of logic. But Abe held it back until they got to Cyrano's nest and Ilya poked at it with his rifle. Cyrano came out and Ilya aimed. "Go!" Abe had screamed, and Cyrano took off like a shot. Ilya still got off two shots. One clipped Cyrano. The little Skullron made it to the wall and over it, back out into the Wilds.

"He's not going to make it very far," said Ilya with satisfaction. "I took off one of his legs." He held up the tiny foot with its bloody end. "Likely to bleed to death out there, unless an Arcwolf tracks him down first. Burn those rags, no 'Cycling allowed. Filthy rat creatures are full of radiation and disease."

The next day at border school Fat Abe became Fat Abe the Mutie Lover. None of the Free cadets would talk to him. Most of the other 'Cycler kids had been sent into the city to more academic boarding schools. But Abe's parents Frankie and Sophie King had this crazy idea that 'Cyclers and Frees should live together. So Abe learned to live with his head in an old 'Cycler book or on his 3D mechanical workbench. He was so miserable his mom had tried to talk to his dad about moving, swapping with another thermal 'Cycler engineer in another sector a hundred clicks along the Border. But Franklin King refused to leave his precious thermal generators and null suit research. He believed that integrating 'Cyclers and Frees was the right thing to do. That's why both he and Ilya supported the border school integrative directive. Who cared if his son had no friends and no chance to ever make any? All dad cared about was the generators.

So Abe started learning everything he could about the thermal generators, the multiple safeties for the steam pipes, and the electrical production coils. Everything that his dad knew and loved. Maybe then his dad would see Abe as more important than some mass of wires and hissing exhaust.

Last night had been Abe's first solo mission. Just a standard uplink problem. Probably corrosion in the couplings, which it had been. The rain up from the south was murder on those couplings, even when you sealed them. Lucky it was an easy fix.

But having Ellie along with him on guard duty, radiating her hatred and disgust of him and all things 'Cycler, had thrown off Abe's rhythm. Just as he was finishing he'd dropped one of the old couplings in the dark and had to fish around for it. Then he'd straightened up and stared straight into the eyes of an Arcwolf. A big one, with a scar stretching down from its left chest all across its neck. It should have been too dark to see its eyes, but the Arcwolf was giving off enough static electric sparks to generate a glow. The electricity was the Arcwolf's way of balancing its own internal overactive electrical system, and Abe's mom thought it was a display of dominance like a bird's mating plumage. To Abe, it felt like the Arcwolf was staring through him, all the way into his deepest secrets. It lowered its head in a sign of greeting and challenge, and Abe had responded naturally by bowing his head, rolling over, and submitting. Afterward, he'd thought about it, but at the time it was the most natural thing in the world. Just putting all his reading and his mom's research into practice.

Then Ellie had shot the Arcwolf. Abe still felt rage at her stupidity. He shoved the hex wrenches to the side of the box and started sorting them by size. Finding the one he wanted was impossible otherwise.

The Arcwolf hadn't been a real threat. It had only been scouting, just looking at this part of the border over before going back over the wall. If she'd just waited, it would have been gone in a moment. He wasn't sure how he knew it was scouting. Again, it just felt reasonable to him. Probably something he didn't quite remember reading about its behavior.

Abe had been scared for the Arcwolf, but it hadn't seemed hurt, just angry. Had Abe heard a metallic clang from Ellie's shot. He'd seen it go for Ellie. Again, without thinking, he'd gotten between the Arcwolf and its prey. He tried to mimic the long-short-long crooning howls of the hurt Arc pup recording he'd heard, but he could tell it wasn't working. The Arcwolf would accept his submission, but not his defiance. Abe was preparing to get attacked when the whistles came from the other side of the wall. Three long and a short, the call to rejoin the rest of the pack. But they'd been whistles, not howls. Someone on the other side of the wall had been calling the Arcwolves back to the pack.

Then Abe had gotten stuck on top of Ellie because his darn hex key wrench somehow found its way into one of her belt loops. He picked one up into the light. Was this the right one? Nope.

Abe had just gotten free of Ellie when he got hit on the side of the head. He'd learned to go limp when he got hit, usually because it terrified his attacker. But Ilya would have just kept hitting Abe because he thought Abe was molesting his daughter. Abe had seen him get in a rage before, beating one of his men so badly he ended up in the hospital. So Abe played dead while Ellie tried to explain what had happened. Abe believed her when she said that she'd hit the Arcwolf. She was insanely good with a rifle. That meant the Arcwolf had recovered almost instantly from a shot to the heart. There were reports that it had happened before, but nobody really believed them. Linesmen shooting in the dark, and not finding the Arcwolf they thought they'd hit. So much easier to think they'd missed. But Ellie didn't miss. Abe didn't want to think about what that meant. He was still trying to come to terms with someone calling the Arcwolves back.

Could a Wanderer survive on the other side of the wall? No, the radiation levels were too high. So if not a Wanderer, what was out there? Abe picked on through the hex wrenches.

Finally, the right match hex key. Abe stuck it into his tool belt, sliding it into its housing coil. He felt complete again. Carefully, Abe checked every pocket of his tool belt one more time to make sure everything was in its place. On a bad night, he'd have to come down to the workshop again in bare feet just to touch everything three times to make sure everything was in its place before he could fall asleep. Abe had a feeling this was one of those nights. He sighed and trudged up the stairs to his room.

At border school the next day, Ellie didn't speak to Abe. He tried to ask her about last night, but she turned her back on him and walked into the bathroom. She was so stupid because he could support her alibi. The few other 'Cycler kids at the school would be on his case for getting together with one of the uptight Free girls. So they'd both get teased. But teenage girl Frees were also supposed to be saving themselves for a marriage contract and weapons exchange, so Ellie would get ten times the grief Abe would. It also sounded like her dad was planning some kind of punishment besides hitting her. But maybe she wanted to be punished. It seemed like a macho Free thing. Ellie was always trying to prove how tough she was, so maybe this was just another chance to show it.

4 PLOTTING

Ellie

Ellie waited for four days for Papa to make up his mind about what to do with her. She knew part of the punishment was forcing her to sit in her barracks' room after dinner until lights out. By the second night she felt like she was going crazy.

Ellie always needed to be outside, even when she was little. Especially at night, when she knew the Arcwolves and other mutie creatures were stirring. Just walking the line at night was thrilling. Stuck inside like she was now felt like she wanted to bash her head against the wall. Ellie did jumping jacks and reverse burpie wall climbs until her arms gave out. Lying panting on the ground, she still had to shut her eyes and imagine herself walking the line or she'd start breathing too fast and panicking that the walls were closing in. She slowed her breath, turned over on the concrete floor, and rested her trembling, sweaty arms across her belly.

In Ellie's mind, she could see the sha sector's twin guard towers, armed with automatic machine guns. Too bad they were never on because the sensor arrays were too sensitive. The Frees had found that out the hard way. One of the towers in the epsilon sector had malfunctioned and decided a Free recruit exercise group was an Arcwolf pack. After that massacre, the Frees kept the automatics off and in reserve, a last-ditch defense if the Arcwolves overran the line. Sure, the Dubsee research division was working on a fix for the malfunctioning sensors. But Ilya had shown the other Frees that Dubsee R&D had ranked that fix in priority below a project on how to make the banana flavor in the Dubsee meal bars "more rich and creamy."

So that left the Free patrols to keep the line safe. Every ten minutes a team of Frees would walk every part of the line. They had electronic movement sensors, but radiation could make these malfunction. Ilya wanted a body nearby to check any disturbance. He didn't trust the sensors. Why should he? Word on the recruit massacre still got out to the Tenners. Those dirt-poor, bottom of the two-miler Dubsee kids might have considered becoming Free contract agents. But once they heard they could be gunned down, they requested work in the food processing plants instead of risking their lives on the line with its malfunctioning guns.

Opening her eyes, Ellie felt the walls of her room sliding closer. So she closed them again and imagined walking the line. The rotting pillars, concrete walls, and thermal towers sticking up like mushrooms forming a familiar jumble. The whole overlayer of wire, everything from shiny new coils to crumbling ancient brown strands, looked like the creepers from a jungle scene in an old Beforer vid.

Ellie's breath quieted as she thought about the Wilds beyond the walls. When she'd been younger, she'd spent time up in the guard towers staring out over the Wilds. They were overgrown so thick you could only see a sea of green and brown, punctuated by occasional bursts of bright colors, giant flowers that waved in the radioactive wind. Ilya had told her to study the plants she could see out there until she understood them.

At first, Ellie had stared really hard, thinking that she would get what he was saying. But after a while she got bored and gave up. When she let her eyes drift across the Wilds, different trees and plants started to stand out. She saw a dandelion, but it wasn't the right size. Out here on the border, big dandelions grew maybe a half a met high. But a dandelion out in the Wilds was visible from hundreds of mets away. It must have been huge, taller than Ellie. The trees next to it looked wrong as well, twisted like somebody in pain. They had strange growths on them that looked like a flock of crows. But there hadn't been regular birds for years anywhere in World City Bela, only clones and synthetically grown pets. When Ellie had told Ilya that the Wilds were just wrong, he'd nodded. "Now you know how to recognize a mutie. It's just wrong somehow."

On the fourth day of her punishment, Ilya came to Ellie's barracks room. He told her that she was on probation from central, that she wasn't to see that fat kid again, and that another screw-up like that would cost her patrol rights. He was fully in control of himself, but treated her like any recruit, with her standing at attention and saluting. Ellie still vaguely remembered long, long ago, when he would pick her up and swing her around. Before he became a commander and she was just one more soldier he was responsible for making strong. "We need you on patrol tonight with Sven. Demetri ate something that didn't agree with him. Probably his wife's cooking."

Ellie tried not to smile. Ilya paused. Ellie thought about asking Papa to question Fat Abe, but she knew he'd expect "her boyfriend" to support her story. So it wouldn't do any good. Besides, for Papa, this wasn't much of a punishment. Ellie was relieved.

As he was leaving, Ilya turned. "Oh, I told Todd about your behavior. Can't have you sneaking around behind his back. A man like Todd deserves to know the truth."

Ellie felt her gut clench as a wave of panic rolled over her. She tried not to throw up as she realized this was the real punishment. Todd wasn't a forgiver. He would end everything between them.

It was the worst thing Papa could have done. Telling Todd she was fooling around on him meant that they were through. "You don't get second chances on the line," that was Todd's motto. It made him a great border guard, but a lousy boyfriend. No, that wasn't true. He'd been a great boyfriend. But it was done. In a second, her life was over. She wanted to scream. But she was a Free soldier, and Frees didn't scream even if you ripped off their arms. Ellie bit down hard on the inside of her cheek, tasting blood, and clenched her jaw until she saw spots. She wouldn't break, wouldn't show Papa she was weak.

Ilya was watching from the doorway. "Good," he turned away. "You can handle not getting what you want. There might be hope for you yet. But you must clean up your mistakes. Get rid of the garbage. Prove yourself a true Free."

Clenching her fists, Ellie tried not to hate Papa. He was right, wasn't he? Papa was following the Free rules, being straight with a fellow Free. But only because he didn't believe her. Papa thought she was some kind of line floozy. These semi-wanderers who traveled from sector to sector after their own sectors cast them out. They were officially forbidden but tolerated as long as they didn't make trouble. How could he think that she was capable of that, and with a 'Cycler like Fat Abe? It made her so angry she could spit or beat someone up.

Fat Abe. 'Cycler garbage. Ellie knew Papa only allowed the integrated border school because he wanted Free cadets to learn all the 'Cycler jobs. He needed to make sure the line could run after the Frees got rid of all the 'Cyclers. His dream was a border society clean of the corruption of Dubsee employees.

That's what Papa meant about cleaning up her mistakes. Fat Abe was her problem, the garbage between her and Todd. Ellie wanted to go right out and punch Abe's smug, know-it-all 'Cycler face. He'd caused this with his stupid wolf howls and sweaty body. But she breathed deep, the way she'd seen Papa do when someone was irritating him to the point of violence. The rage quieted, got cold, and directed. Fat Abe would pay for what he'd done to her, but in a way that wouldn't cause an incident report or cost her patrol privileges. It couldn't be just a beating. She had to make it clear that they'd never been together. Abe had to disappear. Ellie breathed in her rage. Fat Abe would go missing. Ellie would clean up her garbage. She would prove herself to Todd, to Papa, and to all the other Frees.

5 BULLIED

Abe

Abe's life had become unbearable. He'd thought the only people who would know about the misunderstanding with him and Ellie would be local sha sector Free kids. But someone had told Todd, and Todd had put the word out to his friends to get Fat Abe. It seemed like all the Frees in sha sector were Todd's friends.

The Free cadets had always hassled Abe, but since the incident with Ellie even full-grown linesmen had muscled him into corners, sucker-punched him, and told him if he ever touched her or any other Free girl again they'd gut him for the wolves. Even Free women had spit openly in his food in the mess hall. He'd crossed some invisible line, one that made him less than human, an animal only fit for extermination.

For the first time, Abe wasn't just harassed, he was really afraid. He had stopped going out after dark. Abe avoided any hallway that wasn't already crowded. It affected his nerves. Three times every night he'd get up to check his tool belt, and he'd started washing his hands more than the two times he usually allowed for normal cleanliness. Abe's mom Sophie had noticed, and was mentioning medication again, leaving literature about the "Great Things Pharma Division Can Do For You" on a tablet on Abe's bed.

It got so bad Abe thought about telling his dad about the problem. As if it would do any good. The one time Abe had told his dad Franklin about the mutie lover insults before, the "accidental" shoulder bumps in the mess room, Franklin had told him to let it go. Maybe it was because Abe's whole family were all called mutie lovers.

The Kings had carried the mutie loving label ever since Abe's mom Sophie and his crazy uncle Gabriel had tried to really study the Arcwolves. They thought the Arcwolves could be used in some way instead of just exterminating them. Uncle Gabriel had been fascinated by the sparking and thought it could be a power source. The Arcwolves had repaid his interest by carrying Gabriel off and eating him. Since then Sophie had limited her research to tracking Arcwolf sightings on the ancient security camera system of the border wall. So long before Abe got called mutie lover to his face for Cyrano he'd heard the whispered comments about his family in the halls.

The Frees also hated the King family because the King twins had both been allowed to live and granted employee status. Both Franklin and Gabriel were made full employees because of their efforts to increase thermal energy production. With the one-child policy, Nana King had given birth to the twins at home. She kept Franklin a secret, hiding him in a false-backed closet while Gabriel went to school. When he got home, Gabriel would teach his twin what he had learned. It went on until they were both grown. Then they jointly published papers on coupling efficiency, and both got waivers from Central to remain on the line as employees. Every Free woman wished she could have had more than one child. So the Kings parading around as living twins had turned the Frees against them before they did any mutie loving.

It had gotten better for a while after Gabriel's death. Free patrols never found Gabriel's body, even though Abe's dad had begged for them to keep trying. Dad wasn't just sentimental, Abe knew. His dad just wanted the null suit prototype Gabriel had been wearing. After his death, Gabriel's null suit work was mysteriously erased from all the public border databases. All these years later dad was still trying to redo Gabriel's research on converting radiation into electrical energy.

There was an old picture of Gabriel stuck above Franklin's workbench. Whenever Franklin was lost in thought about a problem, he would stare up at the picture of his twin. But when Abe asked about Uncle Gabriel, dad always brushed him off. The only thing he'd say for sure was that Gabriel hadn't been crazy, and Abe should never believe that he was. It was never a good time to ask about Gabriel, it was never "relevant to the task at hand." That was Franklin's favorite phrase, which stopped Abe whenever he tried to talk about the border kids or anything that might be unpleasant. It seemed like there was never a time when Abe's life would be relevant to the task at hand.

Now Abe needed someone to talk to about the Free abuse and he found himself staring at the picture of Gabriel above his dad's workbench. The face was so familiar, but different. Something about the eyes, just a hint of a smile. Like Gabriel knew something he wasn't telling. Abe wished his uncle was still alive to talk to about the Frees. He bet Uncle Gabriel would have some good advice.

Abe fiddled with the thermal array he was rebuilding. Uncle Gabriel was dead, but that didn't mean he was gone. There must be some record in the database. Abe pushed the array away and brought up the workstation surface interface. He found that all of Gabriel's research on the Arcwolves was still in the 'Cycler border database. Abe read everything Gabriel wrote that he could find. A lot of it matched what his mom had written, but Gabriel was convinced the Arcwolves were even smarter. Abe found one old vid of an Arcwolf they'd managed to capture alive. It sat in its cage and looked at the camera like it knew what it was. Abe was so lost in staring at the screen he didn't hear the trudging footsteps behind him.

"Is that thermal array ready?" Abe's dad Franklin came up behind Abe. "What are you watching? *Arcwolf In Captivity*? How is that relevant to the task at hand?"

Abe reached up to turn it off, then stopped himself. He wouldn't be shut down this easy. "I'm worried about the Arcwolves being able to disrupt our repairs." He turned to look at his dad. "If what happened to me is any indication, the Arcwolves are becoming harder to kill."

Surprisingly, Franklin nodded. "Yes. That's been an ongoing issue for some time." He reached past Abe and rapidly clicked through several screens until he came to a border guard set of memos on, "Isolated Resistance of Mutated Specimens." Each one seemed to be a case report of a border guard reporting a partial shot or even what they'd thought was a killing shot of an Arcwolf who had gone back over the wall. Abe scanned down through them and even saw a reference to a scar. Maybe it wasn't all Arcwolves, just the one with the scar. He scrolled back up the memos. They were all dated this year and showed a progression from sector to sector along the length of the wall.

"He's spying." Abe sat back in his old hover chair that tilted a bit to the left and wobbled under his weight. "The Arcwolf is spying on us."

Franklin laughed. "That sounds interesting, but not relevant. Let's get this array ready for use."

When Abe got to border school the next day, someone had hacked his 3D workstation. When he turned on the power, "'Cycler slut" appeared in fat block letters suspended above his station, and then the letters started doing obscene things to each other. It was too slick a job for any of the Free cadets, so it had to be one of the few other 'Cycler kids, probably Isaac. Abe knew the other Cycler kids were mad. They thought he'd crossed the line. Messing around with a Free was like messing around with an Arcwolf. They were the enemy, and you didn't, what was it, fraternize with the enemy? 'Cyclers dated 'Cyclers, Frees married Frees. Frees didn't date, period. So 'Cyclers certainly didn't date them. Abe rebooted his station, erasing the hack. Great, now everyone hated him. They had to move, get out of the sha sector. He was going to talk to his dad. Every nasty Free encounter that day cemented his resolve.

Abe went to see his dad in his workshop as soon as he got home, but

Franklin was elbow deep in some goop, muttering to himself about mitochondria. When dad got like this all that happened when you asked him a question was an angry, "What?" and then a lecture on whether or not the question was relevant to his research. It was his dad's way of telling you to get out, it just took longer. Abe lost his nerve and walked back out of the workshop.

There was a time before dinner, so Abe thought about looking up the other 'Cycler kids Isaac and Ishmael. Sure, they'd give him hell, but it would get it out of their systems and maybe things could go back to normal. They wouldn't be friends, but they wouldn't hate him.

Not right now, Abe decided. He didn't have the energy to tell them over and over that nothing happened until they let him go. All 'Cycler kids thought Free girls must be closet demons in the bedroom because of all that repressed emotion. Abe figured none of the 'Cycler guys had ever actually dated a Free girl. Or a 'Cycler girl, for that matter. The two 'Cycler guys he knew were still at the "theoretical" dating stage. It was a lot less scary to talk about who they might date than to ask and get rejected.

Abe decided to get some of his extra homework done before dinner instead. Most of the 'Cycler kids didn't get educated on the border but boarded in the city because Abe's school was dumbed down for the Free cadets. So for most of Abe's life, he'd done border school and then come home to his mom for a couple of hours of homeschooling on circuits or Beforer history. Abe started on his work but soon got distracted by searching for more data on the Arcwolves compiled by Sophie King.

Abe's mom Sophie was a uber-geek, a super nerd, someone who compiled data for fun and cross-referenced all the security cameras of sha sector in her spare time. Sophie particularly loved stories about Beforer animals, particularly wolves. She'd helped his uncle Gabriel with his Arcwolf research, and in her job as the Sha Sector Thermal Array Inspector still ran reports of every Arcwolf sighting along the border. None of the working security cameras had covered the specific thermal tower Abe had been fixing, but Sophie had still cataloged Abe's encounter as a "possible sighting." She hadn't said anything to Abe about it, just brushed his head and ruffled his hair where Ilya had hit him. If Abe wanted to talk, she'd listen. But she never pushed.

It was Sophie's data that Abe read now telling him about Scar, and her careful analysis of the spotty Border surveillance tapes that gave them some clear shots of the Arcwolf. Her analysis confirmed it was Scar who had been seen up and down the line.

Sophie wrote her remarks to Central with a tone of reverence about the resilience of the Arcwolves. Abe learned more from her comments about the lethal levels of radiation that seeped up in places in the Wilds, through multiple cracks that had opened in ancient containment vessels. Somehow the Arcwolves lived out there, thriving in the deadly environment. Generations of wolves had fed on the prolific Skullrons, bred, and died. Over time the ones with the longest fur and the most active metabolisms had bred into a distinct species that generated enough internal electrical charge in different body areas to give off visible sparks when enraged. Sophie speculated that the wolves' innate fear of fire had made this group rapidly dominant, out-hunting and out-breeding their non-sparking cousins. Alpha males were generally the brightest sparking members of any pack.

No human could survive in the Wilds. Abe knew it. But something who sounded human had whistled for Scar. If they were human, then they'd figured out how to survive out there in the radiation. It would change everything, open up the Wilds for exploration, even settlements. Free up the 'Cyclers to create new energy sources and repair the old ones.

Living in the Wilds, self-sufficient and free of Dubsee, was the dream of 'Cyclers all along the line. They could harvest the heat gradients for power along the edge of the Wilds. But they'd never managed to find a way to harness the radiation and render it harmless. It was what Gabriel and Franklin had spent their lives working on. Abe's dad said Gabriel had a working prototype that could have changed everything before he disappeared.

If Abe could make contact with the whistler, start a dialogue with whoever lived in the Wilds, he could learn how that person survived. Abe could get that secret and give it to the others. He'd be a 'Cycler hero.

Abe leaned back in his hoverchair and crossed his arms behind his round head. Hero Abe. It made Abe feel a little giddy. Once he was a hero, everything would be different. Abe imagined even the Frees giving him grudging respect. Of course, they'd no longer be necessary, because the 'Cyclers would tame the Wilds and create a new utopia. Abe was sure the Frees could be recycled as miners on the Asteroid belt. They wouldn't be wasted, just off-planet. He imagined what it would be like to live without a single Free. No one pushing him, no one hassling him. Living as a hero surrounded by a community of 'Cyclers who all recognized his genius. All he needed to do is find the whistler, to make contact.

But to make contact, Abe would have to go over the wall. And to go over the border wall, Abe needed 'Cycler overseer permission, Free commandant permission, and a bodyguard.

Getting 'Cycler permission wasn't impossible. The good thing about dad ignoring him meant that Abe could probably get his dad to sign something just to get rid of him. Once he got 'Cycler approval the Frees wouldn't care. They'd OK the trip even if Abe was planning to feed himself to the Arcwolves. Some of them would probably help him.

But for the trip to be approved by Central back in the city Abe still needed a Free to volunteer to be his bodyguard, to do babysitting duty on the far side of the border wall. The Frees lived for their border patrols, so it had to be a

Free who wasn't assigned a current patrol duty. Back years ago, they'd had reserve Free guards, but not in Abe's lifetime. Now most of the wives pulled a patrol shift if their man was sick. Abe needed someone crazy enough to go over the wall with him who also didn't have current patrol duty.

Once they got over the wall, Abe had to convince that same Free bodyguard to go find the whistler with him. If they were going to break off from their assignment and go looking for the whistler, that bodyguard had to have nothing to lose. To risk court-martial, a Free would need a huge chip on his shoulder. Someone who really need to prove himself as a Free bad enough that he was willing to risk it all for a chance to be a hero along with Abe. The only person crazy enough might be Todd, who claimed to have stabbed an Arcwolf to death with his bare hands after his rifle jammed. But Todd was working the line on regular duty in che sector. And Todd probably wanted to kill Abe for messing with his girlfriend. So Todd was out. Who else had a chip on his shoulder?

Not his shoulder, her shoulder. Abe needed Ellie. She would understand why he wanted to go look for the whistler because she was the one other person who knew he wasn't crazy. Ellie had nothing to lose. Abe had heard a couple of Free women talking about how Ellie's boyfriend Todd had broken up with her. For a 'Cycler girl, that would have been no big deal. 'Cyclers broke up all the time. But for a Free girl to get dumped was like a full divorce. Ellie was considered tainted, so she would have a hard time getting someone else to court her. Unless she was a hero.

If Ellie was a hero like Abe, she'd have her pick of any Freeman on the line. Even "Six Gun" Sam, the Free celebrity in the zeta sector who could shoot a Skullron through the eye at five hundred mets. Shooting a harmless Skullron seemed like a stupid, sick thing to do to Abe, but Sam was the youngest sector leader just past Abe and Ellie's age. Sam had a fan club among the Free girls, who had his image stamped into their personal gun handles and would sleep with him under their pillows. If Ellie joined Abe and they were successful, she could even date "Six Gun" Sam. If Abe could just get a chance to talk to her, he was sure she'd see how this was her one chance to redeem her life.

Yep, Abe was decided. He would somehow convince Ellie to join him in his search for the whistler.

6 STYMIED

Ellie

Once Ellie had secretly decided Abe must die, she put all of her determination into how to make it happen. The best thing would be to do it off base. Everywhere along the border there were security cameras. Most of them were spotty and there were gaps, but Ellie knew Abe's mom Sophie handled the security footage to check for thermal failures. If Ellie did anything that got caught by any of the cameras, Sophie would find it.

How could Ellie get Abe off base? Maybe if she broke something big, something the 'Cyclers had to go into the city to get fixed? But breaking something that big meant really avoiding any security cameras. Destroying border property could be considered sabotage of the Free protection mission, even if it was a 'Cycler relay station. Sabotage was treason, and treason was a shooting offense. Papa wouldn't order her shot, would he? But he'd have to give the order to show he didn't play favorites. Ellie decided it couldn't be breaking something.

There were other reasons the 'Cyclers went into the city. They were employees, so they had to go discuss the border energy production at meetings with higher-level employees at Central. But Ellie had no assurance Abe would ever be chosen to go.

The problem was that Abe wasn't really a 'Cycler golden boy. Most of them loved being as scruffy as possible. They let their hair grow and let their recycled, scrap-matte clothing fall into rags before they recycled them again. Abe recycled his coveralls every time they got torn. His toolbelt equipment was in perfect, almost Free level condition. Abe didn't even have a beard, shaving it against all 'Cycler custom and showing off his naked chin like a Freeman. It was a nice, strong chin too. In some ways, it was too bad Abe wasn't a Freeman because he wasn't bad-looking. Not really that fat, either.

He was way too clean-cut to represent the 'Cyclers at a city meeting.

Ellie shook herself. Losing Todd had made her so desperate she'd even started mooning after Fat Abe. She must be losing it.

If Ellie couldn't kill Abe on base, and she couldn't be sure of getting him off base into the city, where did that leave her? Maybe she should join Gladys, her Mama, working every day in the barracks pantry. If she was in the pantry Ellie could try and poison Abe. But if she was discovered, that would definitely be treason. And there was no way to get food to just Abe. She'd have to poison a whole sack of flour or a big bucket of beans.

So that left Ellie..nowhere. She grunted in frustration. In the backroom of the pantry, Ellie had been lifting sacks of flour for Gladys, so no one noticed the grunt. Ellie took out her frustration by punching a flour sack until Gladys called back to her, "Easy! If you pop one of those bags, there'll be flour everywhere! You know your father likes everything to be inspection ready at all times!" Ellie didn't care. She gave the bag a dozen more savage punches that left her knuckles imprinted on its sides.

Abe

Abe wasn't sure how to approach Ellie. He knew there would always be other Frees around. Those Frees would never let a 'Cycler talk to a Free girl without chaperoning, which was the same as eavesdropping.

So Abe couldn't come out and tell her. But he had to try and sell Ellie on the idea at the same time.

Abe came up with a plausible cover story and approached Gladys in the pantry in the hopes that Ellie would be working in the back. Of the two parents, Abe preferred dealing with Gladys over Ilya. Ilya would probably just punch him before abe said a word.

Even at her age, Gladys Patton was imposingly beautiful. She had a way of making everything seem graceful. Her eyes were deep and striking, drawing in a person's gaze like a whirlpool. Now Gladys stared at Abe frozen in the sliding doorway of the pantry with those icy brown eyes. Avoiding that dark stare, Abe squared up and wandered into the pantry as if he belonged there. It was a trick Abe had watched his mom do a million times. Sophie would march into a roomful of men and stand like she should be there until the men eventually ignored her and kept talking about whatever they'd been discussing. Abe had never tried it before because he was Fat Abe, someone who belonged nowhere. But now Abe could see himself as Hero Abe, just a glimmer off in the distance of his mind, so he walked into the pantry as if he belonged.

Gladys made a point of serving all the other Free cooks while ignoring Abe. But when there was a lull in the customers, she looked Abe up and down. "You want some old flour sacks to upgrade your clothes?"

Abe didn't take the bait. "Could I please speak to Elizabeta Patton?"

"You'd be apologizing to her for costing her everything?" Gladys kept her voice flat, but Abe felt her anger like a cold wind.

"Yes, ma'am," Abe had already decided he would agree to anything to get a chance to talk to Ellie.

"Ellie!" Gladys called into the back room."Some 'Cycler wants to ask your pardon."

"What?" Ellie came out of the backroom. Abe noticed her knuckles were bloody. Was she killing animals with her bare hands in the back? Abe didn't doubt she could do it. Probably strangling baby Skullrons in her spare time to keep fit. He watched the muscles ripple under her thin, sweaty shirt and wondered if she could kill him with her bare hands. Then he realized Ellie and Gladys were just standing and looking at him.

"I'm sorry," Abe heard how awkward his own voice sounded. "I'm sorry for giving your father the wrong impression and...for everything that happened as a result. If I could do it again, I guess I'd let that Arcwolf attack you because it might have been preferable, but..." Abe could see Gladys trying to break in with a question and hurried on, "...my dad wants me to put new sensors up on the other side of the border wall. I need protection, and I thought you could use an assignment."

Ellie looked like she wanted to kill him.

"I thought it couldn't hurt to ask?" Abe took a couple of steps back.

Gladys put her hand on Ellie's arm.

"Dochka, is what he says about the Arcwolf true? You weren't just messing around with this boy? Was there really a threat?"

Ellie tore her arm away. "Yes, Mama! I tried to tell Papa but he didn't believe me. He sure wasn't going to believe my 'Cycler boyfriend here!" She shoved out her hand, pointing at Abe like she was trying to punch him in the throat.

Gladys pursed her lips. "But I believe you. We're not done with this, it's not right..."

Ellie gripped herself with both arms. "It's done, Mama. Todd doesn't give second chances." She looked like she was going to fold in on herself, then she straightened. Her mouth bent into a smile as if it hurt her. "Yes, Abe. I'd be happy to be your bodyguard on the far side of the wall. When do we start?"

Of all the responses Abe had expected, this wasn't one of them. He started explaining the benefits of the mission, how it would be a good career move for Ellie, until Ellie held up her hand. "I said I'll go. When do we leave?"

Abe's mind raced. "Tomorrow? At dawn." He tried to make it sound like he had a plan. "I'll meet you here, to get our day's rations. We'll spend the day putting in sensors. It'll be...fun?"

Ellie saluted him like a commanding officer. "I'll see you in the morning, sir." The person who had been in agony was gone. Ellie was all cold efficiency. It was like she wasn't even in her body anymore.

Abe left feeling elated and...scared? Was he just scared about crossing the border wall? Or was he scared because he was lying about permission? Or was it that he was scared of Ellie? Abe laughed at himself. Here he was getting exactly what he wanted, and all he could worry about was the possibility of failure. Now all he had to do was to get dad to agree to his mission. Abe walked back to the workshop and thought about how to make it "relevant to the task at hand."

Franklin was working on null suit designs when Abe found him. Even from a distance, Abe could see his father was in a terrible mood. As he came closer, Abe could hear Franklin muttering to himself about resistors.

"Hey dad," Abe stuck his hands into his coveralls and jingled his work belt tools with his thumbs.

"What?" Franklin didn't look up from the diagram. Good, he wasn't listening

"Is it OK if I work on putting sensors up tomorrow? It may take all morning." Abe made himself sound bored like he wanted his dad to say no so he could get out of it.

"Hmmm? Yeah, sure." Franklin had just found something on the diagram and was blowing up the screen to see it better.

"OK," Abe tried to keep his voice calm. "I'll just check out the excursion equipment then. A couple of forms to sign." He held out a tight wad of forms for his dad to initial. Franklin signed them all quickly without looking.

"Good, good," Franklin was ignoring Abe again, trying to fit the small piece in his hand into the diagram on the screen.

Abe walked slowly toward the door. Two steps before freedom, Franklin called, "Hey, Abe."

Abe jumped. He turned back even though he didn't want to. "Yeah?"

Franklin looked up at him. "Be careful out there."

Abe nodded. "Will do." His dad went back to looking at his diagram.

It wasn't far to the 'Cycler supply depot. The regular day packs and gear were patched and worn, but the emergency supply packs were crisp and new. As emergency supplies, they had to be recycled and regenerated every year. Abe selected one of these, resisting the urge to check all its seams or to zip the zippers three times to make sure they worked. He lost the second battle and relaxed into the sound of the zippers slipping back and forth until his mind quieted.

Abe got ten motion sensors. They came with clear boxes that gradually turned cloudy and brown in the rains. When Abe had been younger he'd used a belt sander to grind the sensor covers back to shiny newness. Even now when he signed for the sensors, Abe could still smell the tangy, tickly sensor dust smell in his nose.

7 A MIRACLE?

Ellie

It was complicated to feel grateful to someone you were going to kill. Ellie didn't do complicated, so she focused on the plan.

At first, Ellie thought they'd just go over the wall and she'd shoot Fat Abe. Simple, not too many moving parts. But the clean-up would be awkward. They'd expect a body. No matter what she said about Arcwolves there'd be an inquiry. Inquiries involved Central in the city. Employees at Central judging Free contractors. It never went well for the Frees.

So now Ellies' plan was to wing Fat Abe at the first sign of an Arcwolf. Shoot him in the leg and fall back as the Arcwolf savaged him. Then dispatch the Arcwolf and bring back Abe's body. An Arcwolf attack with a mauled body meant no inquiry. Ellie liked it. She marched down the hall toward evening mess with her newly clean rifle.

Gladys had gotten Ellie's rifle and all the gear she'd need as a bodyguard past the wall. Checked it all out for Ellie and signed in Ilya's name. Stared down the quartermaster when he even thought about questioning the extra ammo and rations.

Then Gladys had surprised Ellie. She said they wouldn't bother Ilya with Ellie's mission. "Keep your gear in the closet until he goes out on patrol," Gladys told Ellie. It was the closest thing to a rebellion Ellie had ever seen in her Mama.

"Won't he be mad when he finds out?" Ellie had asked, half-expecting Mama to change her mind and back down. Once Ilya knew about the mission he'd likely assign someone else, a line soldier, anyone but his disgraced daughter. Going to the far side of the wall was a privilege that Ellie hadn't earned.

But Gladys shook her head. "If what the 'Cycler boy said is true, then your father rushed to judgment. I'll ask Sophie to go over the security recordings. We'll see if there's any proof of what you say. There's no need to compound your father's mistake by giving him a chance to make it worse. If it comes up, I've got a few things to say about casually destroying my daughter's future without good cause. You let me worry about him. You get your rest. You need to be sharp in the morning."

So now Ellie felt grateful to Abe even as she imagined him being savaged by an Arcwolf. If he hadn't spoken up, she'd never have gotten Mama on her side. Without Mama, Papa would never have let her go. So dumb ol' Abe had set himself up for his own doom. Typical 'Cycler overconfidence, Papa would say. Abe was going to die, nice chin and all. Ellie shouldered her rifle and headed down to mess.

Ellie came around the corner of the hall to the evening mess hall, and nearly ran into Todd. Todd was with two of his buddies in uniforms from the che sector. The three of them had surrounded Abe in the hallway, just out of sight of the mess hall doors.

Todd was talking low to Abe, but with his quiet threat voice. "...any 'Cycler talking to any Free girl openly. So I want you to know it's not personal. I'm just holding up Free standards."

For his part, Abe had slumped into a faint but was being held up by Todd's friends.

"I know you can hear me," Todd cracked his knuckles, "and I want to make sure you let all your 'Cycler friends know that Free girls are off-limits." He punched Abe so hard in the stomach that both his friends lost their grip. Abe threw up his entire evening meal on Todd's regulation boots. Evidently, carrots and some kind of squash were featured tonight.

"Oh, it just got personal," said Todd. "I'm afraid you're going to have to clean those boots."

"Stop it, Todd." Ellie surprised herself. Todd spun around, smearing vomit across the floor.

"Ellie, what a surprise. Here to protect your boyfriend?" Todd had his combat sneer, the one he got when he was finishing an opponent. Ellie had never realized how ugly it made him look because it had never been directed at her before.

"I said stop it," Ellie could hardly believe what was she was doing. "Leave him alone. He's a 'Cycler in my sector. So he's my responsibility."

Todd slapped her, hard. Ellie's face stung. She saw red, and her ears started to buzz. Todd was still talking, but it sounded like he was talking slower and slower. "How dare you interfere with a commanding officer? I'm going to be promoted, and you don't even have line status. You're nothing but a common…"

Before he could finish, Ellie hit him with her rifle butt, three times, in critical areas. Todd looked surprised that Ellie could move that fast. Then the pain hit him and he folded even as he lost control of his bladder. Both of Todd's friends lunged for Ellie. She handed one her rifle while kicking the other in the throat between his outstretched hands. When his hands went up to his throat she kicked him in his belly, then brought her other knee into the side of his head as he bent double.

Todd's first friend was just figuring out that he should use the rifle on her when Ellie turned to him. She rotated out of the line of fire, grabbing the rifle while sweeping his forward foot out from under him. As he toppled Todd's friend tried to hold onto the rifle, leaving his head unprotected. Ellie dropped with him using her elbow to accelerate his head and neck into the floor. As his head bounced, Ellie twisted her rifle free, straightening and prepared if he rose again. He didn't. Ellie had practiced for years fighting against her Papa. No way she would be beaten by a few new linesmen from che. All three of them lay in Abe's vomit.

Flexing, Ellie felt the shakes that came after a fight. She breathed heavily, wiping her rifle butt clean on Todd's uniform. He groaned.

"Get up." Ellie nudged Abe, who was lying as if dead. "Get out of here. This never happened."

Abe opened his eyes. "But…"

"Shut up," Ellie glanced around for security cameras. "Todd and his che buddies will never admit I took them down. If we say anything you'll end up in an honor duel with one of them. Is that what you want? Head back through the mess hall and get cleaned up. I was never here. See you in the morning."

Ellie walked down the hall away from the mess hall. She'd lost all her appetite. What had just happened? Had she just defended her target? No, she told herself. She'd just defended her honor. Che Frees couldn't come into the sha sector and do what they liked. It was simple. She tried to block out the sneer on Todd's face even as she felt his slap again hot on her cheek.

Abe

Ellie wasn't late, Abe reminded himself. He was early. After yesterday's run-in with Todd Abe had decided the only way he could continue to live in the sha sector was a successful mission. There was no way Todd wasn't going to gun for him after Ellie had gotten involved. Life at the base would be a living hell from now on unless 'Cycler-Slut-Fat-Abe-the-Mutie-Lover became Hero Abe.

Abe had memorized the likely paths beyond the border wall into the Wilds as far as the old line maps would tell him. Most of the maps were from old hunting party scouting trips from a generation ago. Ilya's grandfather, Ezekiah, had done many of them. But there were even a couple of Beforer maps that included street names and building complexes in Abe's mom Sophie's digital archives. They were buried under the Wilds now, but there had once been whole towns with names like Wormwood that gave Abe a shudder to think about finding again. There might be nothing left of the original roads, but Abe memorized them anyway.

Now Abe had an irrational fear that if Ellie didn't come soon he'd forget the maps and lose his way as soon as they crossed the border wall. It was the same fear he had when he was cramming for a border school test and then trying to take it as soon as possible before he forgot what he'd learned. Abe resisted the urge to go find a bathroom and wash his hands until they were sore and red. A little voice inside his head said it might help with the waiting.

"Ready to go, commanding officer?" Ellie's voice made Abe jump. She'd snuck up behind him while he was looking for the nearest bathroom. But when he turned she didn't look happy about her trick. She looked...neutral? For some reason, it gave Abe the creeps. But he told himself this was probably her official persona, the one she'd never showed him before. Maybe this was her way of showing respect? It just made him feel odd, staring at her blank expression like a Beforer doll or a toy soldier.

"Hey, thanks about yesterday…" Abe started.

"Never happened," Ellie was wooden.

"Uh, right." Abe went silent.

Ellie shifted her rifle and tightened a backpack strap. "Ready when you are, sir."

"Right, right," Abe dragged his thoughts back to the map in his mind. It wouldn't do to lose his brain maps wondering about Ellie's face. "From the front of the depot building, we'll go straight through to the first gate, then right to the second. Right again to the third. You've got all the passkeys?"

Ellie slapped her hip. Abe admired her leg pouches. They were snug against her muscular thighs and looked almost like cowboy chaps. He'd thought to muffle his own toolbelt in with his pack's provisions. Abe had gotten enough provisions for five days by going back to the pantry with forged permission slips from his dad. So his pack was much heavier than it should have been for a day trip. But Abe was hoping Ellie didn't know how much 'Cycler gear should weigh.

"Well, lead on," Abe motioned Ellie to lead the way. He wished he had something he could think of to prepare Ellie. Very soon he would need to ask her to leave the line entirely and head out into the Wilds to look for the whistler. But he couldn't think of anything to say. So he just followed in silence through the gates.

8 DEEPER

Ellie

It was perfect, except it wasn't. Ellie watched the border wall from the corner of her eyes and saw all the gaps. From the sha sector side, all the wire and extra layers made it look solid. But from the Wilds side the wall was mostly gone, and the fences were full of holes. Many of them, she noted with disgust, were big enough for an Arcwolf to creep through. It was like the critters were just making the wall their own highway.

But it wasn't much better for stopping humans from seeing this side. Ellie had never thought of just how much of the Wilds she could see through the wall because it was all green and brown. From this side every time she glanced up there was a gap with accusing empty windows overlooking their route. She could practically see all the way back to the barracks. Even if they were between gaps, the automatic guard towers loomed over the line. The cameras up there were mostly busted, burned out by the rains, but Ellie couldn't be sure. If any camera caught her shooting Abe, she might as well just stay out here and take her chances in the Wilds.

If only there was some way to go deeper, to go past the first line of the high bushes and trees. Ellie looked longingly at that covering brush. As little as ten mets into the deep Wilds, Ellie could shoot Abe with no fear anyone on the line could see anything.

Sure, they'd hear the shot. But Ellie could make up any story she wanted..unless Papa decided to investigate. Normally he'd believe one of his own men, but he wouldn't believe Ellie. She needed evidence of an Arcwolf attack, showing that Abe had gotten in the way and she'd had no choice. They might believe she'd missed the Arcwolf and hit Abe, even though Ellie had a shooting range record better than any of them. Only Papa wouldn't believe a woman froze under pressure and shot the 'Cycler she was babysitting. But he'd know she'd taken care of her garbage, corrected her mistake, and stay silent.

Abe

Abe trudged along, regretting the extra food he was carrying. The day was warm even under the perpetually grey sky and Abe was sweating. He stopped to set a sensor and took a water break. All the time he was trying to figure out how to finesse getting Ellie to head into the Wilds. He realized there was no way. Ellie would see through any tricks. The best thing Abe could do is lay out his plan for her. She wouldn't come with him, but maybe she'd let him slip out of range before she set off an alarm flare. It was the best he could hope for.

"Ellie," Abe turned to where she was tailing him.

Ellie held up a fist for silence, listened intently, and then relaxed. "What?"

Abe took a deep breath and blurted, "I think my uncle Gabriel is still alive and training Arcwolves. I want to go look for him out in the Wilds." He swallowed and waited.

Ellie looked at Abe with the strangest expression on her face. "Wait. You want to go out into the Wilds?" She pointed into the brush as if it wasn't clear which way led into the Wilds.

"Well, I know it's a lot to ask. You don't have to go with me. I could just go on my own. But if you could just take your time getting back, give me a chance..."

"Stop," Ellie held up her hand, "I'm going with you."

"Really?" Abe was really grateful but also felt strangely uneasy. "I don't know how to thank you! It really means..."

"Shut up," Ellie looked back at the guard towers. "Lead on."

Abe started weaving his way through the outer fringes of the wall. He started sweeping with his wrist Geiger counter every few minutes even though this close to the wall it should be just background radiation. Abe told himself it was reasonable to be extra cautious, not just him trying to deal with his nerves. No telling when you could hit a hot pocket of radiation from a cave-in.

Why did he feel so nervous? Sure, it was dangerous to head into the Wilds, but Abe was so excited to be looking for some sign of his uncle Gabriel he shouldn't mind. So, why did he still feel so uneasy? The hair on Abe's neck prickled like he was walking into a trap.

9 TRAPPED

Ellie

It was all Ellie could do not to shout with triumph. When she was very young Papa told her a story. One of his ancestors was starving. The ancestor was cleaning his gun, a musket, on the porch. A deer, a Beforer animal hunted for meat, walked right out of the woods and up to the porch. All Papa's ancestor had to do was load his musket slowly and shoot the deer.

That's how Ellie felt now. Her target had asked to walk right into the slaughter zone. Fat Abe had given her the perfect cover. All she had to do now was wait for something to attack him and shoot Abe in the fight.

But even though she couldn't believe her luck, Ellie felt vaguely guilty. Her ancestor all those years ago had killed to feed his family. If he hadn't needed the meat, he'd have let the deer go off back into the wild.

Maybe that would be best. Just let Abe go off into the Wilds without backup. Let him get himself killed. Ellie might be able to say Abe lost her or bolted instead of finishing him herself.

But it would never fly with Papa. He'd know she just let Abe die. It might not bother him, but he'd know. Papa would hold it over Ellie for the rest of her life. She'd never get the respect a Free deserved from him.

Losing a 'Cycler in a firefight with some Arcwolves was understandable. Nobody could fault Ellie for doing her job as best she could. There'd be too many Arcwolves. Nobody could have done it better. Only Papa would know she staged the whole thing to cover for her mistakes, to prove herself a true Free. For the first time in her life, Ellie hoped the Arcwolves were already stalking them.

Abe

How would he find Uncle Gabriel? Or the whistler if it wasn't Uncle Gabriel? Abe had made it past any trace of the original wall. There were still occasional overgrown structures, former outposts of the Frees. Long ago, in Ezekiah's time, they used to take city employees on hunts in the Wilds. The Free hunters would put the employees in one of these buildings so they could shoot the Arcwolves without any risk of getting attacked. The buildings were still solid, so Abe planned to spend the night in one.

But he could only stay out here one night without heading deeper into the Wilds. Otherwise, sha sector might send a search party as deep as they'd gone so far. They'd also send word to Ellie's emergency 'talkie and she would have to respond as long as they were within signaling range. Everyone knew that the Wilds' radiation played havoc with any signaling devices. That's why you couldn't track any of the animals. One animal might look like a dozen, then disappear entirely under the brush, which gave off its own changing heat signatures.

So there was one night to find Uncle Gabriel. But Abe couldn't track down his uncle. Uncle Gabriel had to find them. And he'd only find them once the Arcwolves found them.

As they passed one of the outposts, Abe stopped. "I want to try something stupid." He turned to Ellie.

"That's not a surprise," Ellie didn't even smile. She couldn't meet his eyes and kept glancing back at the trail.

She must be getting tired, Abe told himself.

Ellie followed Abe into the building. It was small, basically a steel cage sunk into the ground with a broad roof to keep off the burning acid rains. The front was a mess of bars with slit holes for the Frees or their employee guests to fire out at attacking creatures.

Abe barred the gate behind Ellie, took a deep breath, and howled. He hit the notes just right, with the tapering end note of challenge. Any Arcwolf within hearing would take that howl as a challenge from a young male Arcwolf. It was the closest thing Arcwolves had to a string of swear words followed by, "Do you think yer man enough?"

"Are you crazy?" Ellie slapped her hand over Abe's mouth, "That sounded real! You could…" she dropped her hand, "bring the Arcwolves right here right now." Ellie turned away to hide her smile.

"Wait," Abe was confused, "are you mad or happy?"

Ellie

"Both," Ellie shrugged, "it's… a girl thing. Deal with it." She was having trouble controlling her emotions. Her admiration of Abe's strategy was struggling with her exhilaration at being so close to ending him and regaining her status in Papa's eyes. Ellie felt sick inside, like right before her moon cycle before she got a patch. So she wasn't lying to Abe. She was both mad and happy.

"Oh, OK," Abe made sure the gate door was barred well.

An answering howl sounded from the depth of the Wilds. Abe answered it before it finished, cutting off the responding challenge. This time Ellie just stood back from Abe and checked her rifle. She made sure her spare ammo packs were easy to hand.

There was a chorus of howls. Abe counted at least six different voices out loud, including..could it be? He said it sounded like the gravelly voice of Scar. Abe had listened to Scar's howl over and over when he found one that Sophie had caught in a security recording.

Given the distance of the howls, the Arcwolves arrived in moments, sliding through the brush of the Wilds like it was made for them. Instead of attacking, the Arcwolves hung back from the gate structure. Ellie sighted one, a younger Arcwolf who was less cautious. She squeezed off a shot. The Arcwolf yelped and went down. Ellie cursed. She had aimed to nick it, just to make it angry. She wanted these Arcwolves to attack Abe as soon as she released the gate door and shoved him out. But she'd instinctively shifted to her kill zone with her rifle as she shot. So the Arcwolf lay still without another sound.

Cursing under her breath, Ellie put another bullet in the chamber. When she looked up, Abe was blocking her view.

"We don't want to kill them," Abe explained it to her like she was a naughty little kid. Ellie resisted hitting him with her rifle butt. "We're waiting for Uncle Gabriel or the whistler to show up." He patted her arm like she was stupid.

Ellie snapped. She saw red and her ears buzzed. People had been telling her what to do all her life, and now even her target Fat Abe was giving her lip. It was like taking advice from a Skullron. She grabbed Fat Abe's thumb in a vicious lock, twisting him double. Then Ellie stuck her rifle in her armpit and hauled him toward the door.

Unlatching the gate, Ellie twisted Fat Abe's hand until he whimpered and stumbled through. He'd gone limp under her hold, which suited her fine. "Go play with the Arcwolves, Fat Abe, you mutie loving bastard!" Ellie aimed a kick at his backside, but Abe had already collapsed to the ground and curled into a fetal position to protect his head outside the enclosure so she missed. Her foot hung stupidly in the air as if to prove she couldn't even do this one thing right. Suddenly the only thing Ellie wanted to do was kick Fat Abe.

Forgetting her training, Ellie stepped out of the protective gate. One kick to the backside wasn't enough. Once she started kicking him, Ellie wanted to kick Abe for everything wrong with her life. It wasn't enough to kick his rear end, Ellie wanted to kick Abe in his stupid face. She moved around his limp body and pulled her foot back. Only then did she hear the rumbling growl.

Ellie looked up into the eyes of the biggest Arcwolf she'd ever seen. The beast had come around the far side of the enclosure so Ellie had missed the fiery sparks coming off the creature's enraged body. Now they stared at each other across Abe's body. The Arcwolf was directly between the enclosure's door and Ellie.

Despite the terror in her gut, Ellie assessed her danger. Jumping over Abe to get to the enclosure would set off the Arcwolf. Running would set off the Arcwolf. If she looked, Ellie suspected other Arcwolves had circled behind her. But looking around would set off the Arcwolf in front of her.

There was one possibility. If Ellie gut-shot Abe, the shot might get the Arcwolf to attack him first. It might give Ellie a chance to get past the Arcwolf and back into the enclosure.

Ellie swung up her rifle. The Arcwolf jumped. Instead of aiming at Abe, Ellie automatically swiveled the rifle toward the Arcwolf. But her grip was wrong. Ellie could tell she was far too slow. The Arcwolf tore into her arm and she went down under it. Ellie's rifle got sprayed with Ellie's blood before it went spinning away. Ellie resisted screaming from the pain as her forearm ripped open from the Arcwolf's teeth.

Nothing but survival was left. Ellie's world shrank to the size of her body and the Arcwolf on top of her. Punching the Arcwolf in the nose got the creature to release her forearm, but when Ellie bent her knees to kick it off the Arcwolf sank its teeth into her thigh. Ellie found herself lifted off the ground by one thigh and shaken. Her head bounced against a rock or a tree root, once, twice. Ellie saw the black fuzzy haze of unconsciousness closing in from the edges of her vision. She vaguely thought she was going to die. That's funny, she thought as she went unconscious, death sounds like whistling.

10 DYING

Abe

Abe was still in the fetal position with his arms over his head. But something small was pulling at his hair. He wanted to move, but he could still hear the big Arcwolf next to him tearing at Ellie.

When the Arcwolf had first gone for Ellie, Abe had almost fought for her. He'd had to remind himself that Ellie had almost killed him. She'd thrown him out of the protective enclosure and kicked him so that every part of his back and legs felt bruised. Even so, only the reality that the Arcwolf would just kill them both made Abe lie still.

But now a small form was pushing its way under Abe's hand and poking at him with sharp little claws. Abe opened one eye to see a strangely familiar furry little face. A Skullron was in his face, its familiar arrow-shaped face marking unmistakable.

"Cyrano?" Abe whispered.

In answer the Skullron burrowed into the top of Abe's coveralls, pushing itself into the hollow of his collarbone like Cyrano had always done when Abe was younger.

Now Abe heard whistling. The Arcwolf was moving off. Abe knew that whistle. He guessed it meant, "Retreat and regroup" because it was similar to the Arcwolves' call before they went back over the wall as a group.

Abe rolled up, wincing, and called out, "Uncle Gabriel!" The Arcwolf was still padding off and ignored Abe as if Abe's voice was branches rustling. "Uncle Gabriel! I know it's you!" Abe waited, but nothing happened. The Wilds were strangely still. "It's little Abe. I came looking for you!"

There was a long whistle, then nothing. Abe heard something rustling through the brush, then an extraordinary creature slid into view. It had to be wearing a null suit, because Abe recognized the same colors and cut that his father Franklin had been working on forever. But this null suit was puckered in the middle, so that it looked like the null suit had grown into the body of the creature. Out of the pucker grew a range of small plants. Several of them had flowers, and as the creature walked in its sliding shuffle the flowers swayed back and forth like questing belly antennas. The facemask of the null suit was still there, but cracked so that Abe could see a small hole in the middle like one black eye staring at him. As the creature moved closer to Abe it lifted the null suit faceplate. Abe could see his father's mirrored face, scarred horribly so that one eye was blinded. It was Franklin's twin brother Gabriel, Abe's uncle.

"W-what's this? W-What's this?" Gabriel mumbled to himself as he approached Abe. "L-little Abey, c-come to me?" He peeked at Abe with his one good eye. "B-best be getting when the g-etting's good, little Abey. Ol' man bear, he's c-coming. Coming soon. S-smells your friend's b-blood on the wind and the little pup she k-killed. Ol' man bear eat y-you up in two b-bites. Yum yum! R-run away little Abey, run away f-fast." Gabriel gestured with his hand and turned away.

"You're alive!" Abe was still trying to deal with finding his uncle.

Gabriel laughed, a hacking sound. "Hah! M-mostly dead. I'm b-busted good! Shot in the head and left for d-dead. Pieces of a null suit in m-my head, little Abey, in m-my area of B-broca. M-makes me s-speak bad. B-but who's ol' Gabey g-going to talk t-to? O-only ghosties and w-wolves out h-here. S-soon G-gabey be a g-ghostie too. Mostly d-dead, only a-alive for revenge on him that d-did it,"

"Who did it?"

Gabriel laughed. "I-Ilya, of c-course. Gut shot and h-head shot me. All for a w-woman. Left me for d-dead. He's gonna die, gonna d-d-die, that man."

At the mention of Ilya, Abe looked over at Ellie. She was unconscious, lying in a pool of her blood as it soaked into the soil. Already the twisted bugs of the Wilds were landing on her and dipping their snouts into her wounds.

Abe scrambled over to Ellie to look at the damage. He winced and staggered from the bruising Ellie had given him. She looked unconscious, but he still approached her cautiously. Her blood was still pumping, and she was breathing shallow breaths.

"L-leave 'er." Gabriel shuffled rapidly past Abe to peer at Ellie. "She g-got maybe ten minutes. Long enough to a-attract ol' man bear. L-long enough to get clear. W-we go now." He tugged at Abe's arm.

"We can't leave her," Abe protested.

"W-we ain't. S-she's dead," Gabriel pulled Abe away.

"But she's Ellie Patton, Ilya's daughter," Abe thought fast. "She'd make great bait."

Gabriel stopped. He shuffled back toward Ellie. "N-no lie? Ilya's g-girl?"

He pulled out

a wicked-looking knife. Abe moved to stop him. Gabriel flicked the knife so that it buried itself between Abe's feet. "G-go!" Gabriel gestured to the far side of the enclosure. "G-gut that lil pup! make a m-messy mess for ol' man bear. I f-fix up Ilya's g-girl." He laughed, a high keening sound. "I fix her up g-good!"

Abe stumbled through the brush until he tripped over the body of the young Arcwolf Ellie had shot. Holding his breath, Abe sawed into its belly. It was tougher going than he would have thought. When he had a good-sized hole, Abe reached inside the fallen Arcwolf and pulled out its guts. It was a relatively healthy Arcwolf, and Abe wondered how many Skullrons it took to feed an Arcwolf this well. He heard branches snapping off in the distance. Whatever was coming was big enough it didn't mind making a racket. Abe staggered back as fast as he could to where Gabriel was hunching over Ellie.

Gabriel looked up at Abe when he came up. "No g-good, lil Abey, no s-saving her with needle and th-thread," Gabriel was wrapping Ellie's arm with strips of what looked like a null suit. Her thigh was already wrapped tight.

"So you can't save her?" Abe looked back over his shoulder, where the crashing was getting louder.

Gabriel laughed. "Not s-save her 'cept to be like m-me. No simple life, just a b-big beastie kept alive by l-little beasties. Not d-dead, not alive. We g-go now!" Gabriel hoisted Ellie up onto his back with surprising ease and shuffled into the brush with Abe following.

Ilya

Ilya turned away from his wife Gladys, "I cannot do that."

"Sure you can, you're the commander of this section," Gladys used her gentle pleading tone on him.

"How's it going to look to my men?" Ilya threw up his hands, "Me breaking my own orders about hunting parties to go fetch my own daughter? She's out there making kissy-face with some 'Cycler brat. Better she gets eaten by Arcwolves than make us the grandparents of some dirty 'Cycler mongrel."

"You don't know that!" Gladys was on the warpath now "Did you ever check with Sophie about the Arcwolf attack before you destroyed our daughter's future with Todd? Did you even think of asking for the security recordings from Sophie before you passed judgment, left our daughter's fate in the hands of Central?"

"Half of those damn cameras don't work, you know that."

"But did you check before branding your own daughter unfit for marriage, maybe only fit for the asteroid belt?"

Ilya was silent. Gladys had never done this to him. In all their years together she'd never questioned his decisions. He was too shocked to be even angry.

"Did you?"

"It wouldn't have made any difference. I know what I saw with my own eyes." What had he seen? A flash of his daughter's white skin burned into his memory. Ilya was done with this conversation. "My judgment is final and my word is the law. Never question me again." He stood up, towering over his wife.

Gladys bowed her head. "Under Free custom, you are right. I will not speak of this again. In silence, I take the only action left to me."

Ilya lost the smile of triumph. "What action?"

"Well, all I can say is that it's going to be mighty quiet in your quarters from now on," Gladys crossed her arms. "Just you, without Ellie and me in it. I'll be sleeping above the pantry till Ellie comes home." She moved toward the door.

Inside Ilya, something was crumbling. Everything he had, everything he knew about what was right and wrong, was centered on his wife. She was the pillar of goodness that made the nightmares and waking nightmares of the border bearable. "Gladys, wait! You know she's probably not alive." Ilya tried to sound calm and reasonable. "It's been a day and a night now. We all heard the Arcwolves howling yesterday, lots of them. Too many for even Ellie with that idiot 'Cycler to protect. They're both Arcwolf chow."

"That may be," Gladys turned. "But I'll tell you this, Ilya Patton. Until I see my daughter's body you'll see no more of mine." She walked out and shut the door on him, but not before he could see the tears streaming down her cheeks.

Ilya slumped into a chair and rubbed his hands through the greying bristles on his scalp. He couldn't ask his men, but he could go himself. It would be dangerous, but without Gladys, the nightmares would come. The nightmares he'd fought since his childhood. Life would be hardly worth living.

Nothing terrified Ilya in the daytime. He'd wrestled an Arcwolf with his bare hands, screaming as the creature shocked him again and again. But in the night Ilya's father came, joined by a shadowy dead man with dark skin and burning eyes. Together they chased Ilya through endless muddy fields toward a border wall that never came closer. Only Gladys could hold him in the night and keep them away. Tonight Ilya would have to stuff his own mouth with his blanket to keep from screaming.

11 ALIVE?

Ellie

Ellie woke up feeling like an Arcwolf had taken a dump in her mouth. At least a couple of Skullron had. She gagged, spat, and coughed.
"Hey!" Abe yelled, "you're spilling your soup."

"It tastes," Ellie's own voice sounded raspy and faint, "like Skullron poop."

"Skullron poop is very nutritious, and one of the least radioactive food sources in the Wilds." Abe sounded defensive. "Besides, how would you know?"

Ellie tried to remember. Her mind was hazy. "Basic survival training for Free cadets includes food scavenging. You never forget that taste," Ellie coughed again.

"Yuck," Abe tried to spoon another bite of soup into Ellie's mouth. She closed her lips and tried to turn her head. It hurt really bad. Ellie started realizing just how much she hurt all over. There were even some new kinds of pain she'd never felt before, which Ellie wouldn't have thought possible.

"I should point out you've been eating this for days," Abe moved the spoon back to the bowl for the moment.

"No wonder I feel like Skullron poop," Ellie coughed again. "How long have I been out?"

"Not sure," Abe looked around them, "we're underground here. At least four or five days if we base it on Uncle Gabriel's habits. Though he's a bit...erratic. It could be twice as long." Abe rolled his shoulders, "The bruises on my back feel about a week old."

Ellie suddenly remembered how he had gotten those bruises. She'd lost it, as bad as any time she'd seen Papa lose it. She'd lost it and there'd been an Arcwolf. Biggest one she'd ever seen. She could see it now biting into her thigh, severing the inner artery and spraying Ellie's dark blood in a gush, lifting Ellie like a limp rabbit to shake her to death. She remembered passing out, giving up. Dying.

"Didn't I try to kill you?" Ellie peered at Abe without moving her head. Had she dreamed the whole thing? No. She hurt too bad. "That Arcwolf got me. I was bad off, I remember…dying. Why didn't you leave me for dead?"

Abe was silent so long Ellie looked to see if he was still there and regretted it as her neck twinged so bad it made her grunt. He was chewing his lip and gazing off into the distance. The blinking lights of the various consoles in the lab room around them lit his face like a sculpture. "I've had a lot of time to think about it."

"I thought about leaving you out there," Abe said at last, "not sure why I didn't. The easy answer is that I'm a 'Cycler. 'Cyclers don't waste things. Certainly not people. I guess part of me thought you were worth saving, just in case." He stirred the soup. "But you tried to kill me, and I guess that's what you were planning all along. If I'd really had time to think about it, I might have left you for the bear. But I just reacted. When I saw you hurt, I wanted to save you. I guess I didn't think it through. I just did it."

Something chittered.

"What's that sound?"

"Oh," said Abe, "it's the craziest thing. Cyrano showed up. He's still alive! He must have been following us from the border wall."

"Cyrano?"

"My Skullron. You remember. The one I showed you and you tried to get killed."

"I had to report you," Ellie defended herself. "You were the one breaking the rules. In my place, you'd have done the same thing."

Abe paused. "Maybe."

Ellie swallowed. "You had time to rethink your decision while I was out. Did you decide to kill me slowly? Are you poisoning me with Cyrano's Skullron poop?"

Abe bristled, then saw the slight smile on Ellie's lips. He sighed. "No, I decided once we brought you back it would be a waste of risking both our lives if you died. Don't flatter yourself that it has anything to do with you. I take professional pride in my work. I finish any project I start, and I do my best."

"So I'm like a busted coupling," Ellie nodded her head and winced.

"More like a blown generator. Uncle Gabriel had to replace a lot of your fluids and rebuild your bone tissue. The Arcwolf took a nine-centimeter section of your saphenous vein, so we had to use null suit fabric to rig up a replacement. You were also missing a big chunk of your left thigh and most of your right forearm. We assumed you wouldn't want to live as a cripple so we rebuilt those parts using the null suit and Arcwolf tissue."

Ellie tried to look down at her body, but her neck hurt too much.

"Then you had a heart attack and a minor stroke. Uncle Gabriel said it was from your massive blood loss. Oh, and a tiny piece of the null suit broke off and got lodged in your neck. So he injected your heart with the last of his expanding drugs and filled you full of Arcwolf blood to keep it running. We also had to cut into your neck to get the null suit bit out. That's why your neck is all torn up." Abe was getting into talking about his details. "I learned a lot from Uncle Gabriel about quick sutures. He let me close up your skin once he'd cleared the blockage."

"Wait, what?" Ellie could suddenly locate her neck pain to the right side of her neck near the base of her head. Now that she was paying attention, Ellie could feel a mass of cloth along the side of her neck.

"I did a running stitch along the side of your neck and closed it..." Abe repeated it like Ellie was a slow learner.

"Yeah, yeah," Ellie interrupted. "Skip back to the part where I get filled up with Arcwolf blood?"

"It's not ideal, I know," Abe stirred Ellie's soup again. "But we're limited here by a lack of resources. This underground lab Uncle Gabriel found abandoned was never stocked for a full surgery and he used up most of the medical supplies on himself when he first arrived. You're lucky. He says the Arcwolf blood only works when there are already null suit biobots in your system. You already had them because the null suit bits from your bandages had broken off and gone everywhere. Otherwise, the Arcwolf's blood's internal radiation would sicken and kill you."

"So I'm part Arcwolf now," Ellie looked hungrily at the soup despite herself, and Abe started spooning it into her mouth again. It wasn't that bad once you got past the texture and the taste. Just like survival school, Ellie told herself.

"The Arcwolf blood was what gave Uncle Gabriel the idea for the null suits." Abe was talking as much to himself now as Ellie. "He saw the internal bacterial species within the Arcwolves' blood as being part of the solution, not just a chronic infection. Imagine, these little bacteria use radiation to power their own internal Kreb's cycle, and even smaller mitochondrial nanobacteria to fuel themselves. It supercharges the repair process of the cells, and the excess builds up in the Arcwolves' organs. When blood is shunted into the fight-or-flight pathway it moves to the outer limbs unevenly. The arcwolves are mosaics with built-in electrical imbalances along the wolf's Blaschko lines. That's why when the Arcwolf is stressed some of it gets discharged as sparks between the hairs of the wolf and the surrounding plants or whatever. It's amazing! Instead of shooting them, we should be harnessing the Arcwolves as a power source! I'm so jealous of you because you're only the second person in the world to use that same radiation to help you live."

Ellie throated another mouthful of nasty soup, "What do you mean?"

She'd only partially gotten some of what Abe was saying, but it felt safer to let him ramble on instead of dealing with the emotions of having him save her life. She'd tried to kill him after she'd blamed him for what happened with Papa. She'd been so full of rage she'd planned to ambush an unarmed opponent. Ellie couldn't stomach who she'd become, the kind of person who would do something like that. Safer to not think about it. Get strong, get better. Emotions could wait until after they got back to the wall and safety.

Abe was looking at Ellie with what, jealousy? "I don't think you heard me. In the history of the world, you're the second person after Uncle Gabriel to harness the power of radiation-absorbing mitochondria directly in your bloodstream. Uncle Gabriel calls them Rams, and says they were first perfected in the many generations of radioactive Skullrons well back in the Beforer times. Scientists back then talked about the resistance of certain species to living in high radiation conditions. But they only looked at DNA changes and rapid recovery from exposure. They never suspected that cellular structures were actually becoming dependent on the radiation to sustain life. Every time they took one of the Skullron's rodent ancestors out of the radiation to study them, the rodent would die. The researchers thought it was due to radiation exposure. No one thought to question if the rodents were dying from a lack of radiation. Uncle Gabriel figured out that they needed that radiation to live. Without it, they were starving. It's like dying of thirst without even knowing you're thirsty."

Ellie swallowed again as she thought. She squared her shoulders and the motion made her cringe with pain. "So I need radiation?"

Abe nodded. "You do. You and Uncle Gabriel are the first humans who can only exist in the Wilds. You need the Wilds' background radiation like food. It makes you stronger instead of weaker. Isn't it amazing? Think of the possibilities!"

"What about you?" Ellie tried to gesture, but her arms wouldn't move and the pain shot up to her head. She grimaced instead.

"Oh," Abe looked sad. "I'm just normal, so I have to wear this null suit. On the way here I absorbed some radiation. Uncle Gabriel said it wasn't enough to kill me so it's not worth it to put me through the risk of infecting me with null suit bits and Arcwolf blood. Besides, we needed all his blood reserves to keep you alive. So I'm stuck being ordinary for now."

Ellie noticed for the first time that Abe was wearing a skin-tight shimmering suit complete with a hood. Seen full length, he really wasn't fat. Just well-rounded, and it suited him.

Abe saw her looking and mistook her critical eye. "Oh, I'm supposed to wear my face mask, but it closes me in so I have trouble breathing. Besides, this bunker is in a low radiation zone. The Frees who outfitted it ages ago found the safest place they could. That's why Uncle Gabriel has to go out every day. He needs to get more radiation. He's been irradiating you here in the lab because he didn't want to rip out all your stitches by moving you. When you're unconscious you could just bleed internally and we wouldn't know. But now that you're awake and your neck has partially healed, maybe we can walk you out?"

Ellie tested her legs. She grunted. "I can't even move my feet."

"Oh, OK," Abe shrugged. "You can't blame me for trying. We can carry you, but you're pretty heavy for a girl, um, woman. A Free woman."

Ellie tried to laugh but thought better of it when her ribs spasmed. "I think the word you're looking for is a female dog. Seriously, why haven't you been poisoning my food? I'm a liability. You owe me nothing. Worse, I tried to kill you. If it was me in your place the only way you'd still be alive is if someone ordered me to keep you alive. I'd at least be spitting in your food."

"Who says I haven't?" Abe grinned. "But I thought it through from your point of view. It helped when I looked at how things turned out for you. I mean, my life was total garbage too, but at least I could look forward to leaving and starting fresh in the city. As a Freewoman, you couldn't get out.

"It's honestly your dad's fault that your life is in the crapper. But it doesn't help that your boyfriend was "one-shot" Todd, a great marksman, and a total prick. He'd never give you a chance to tell your side of the story or forgive you. And that was before you kicked his butt and saved me from a serious beating. So it's their fault you've got nothing.

"But I get that you can't bring yourself to blame either one of your heroes. So it makes sense to blame me. As 'Cyclers we're taught to forgive till it hurts, to never give up on a relationship if it might be saved. But as a Free, you shoot first and bury your emotions later. I don't like it, but I get it.

"You at least had the smarts to wait and try to make it look like an accident. Another Free might have just shot me the next time she saw me. Don't forget when your moment came you didn't shoot me in the back. You just kicked the crap out of me. I've gotten worse from other Frees for far less reason. It doesn't make it right, and I think Frees have serious issues, I'm just saying you reacted normally given that all of you are blood-thirsty psychos."

Abe held up his hand. "I'm not saying I forgive you, and I'm not sorry I left your rifle behind. From now on you walk in front of me. I took the precaution of tying down your arms in case you decided to beat me up again. But I understand your point of view. Crazy, homicidal, and based on insane logic. But I get it."

Ellie bit her lip. Abe got her emotions better than she did. He deserved something, but she had nothing to offer him. Except for maybe the admission that she'd been truly and totally in the wrong. Fighting a life of conditioning, Ellie tore out of herself the one thing that Papa would never say, "I'm sorry."

"Whoa!" Abe looked around. "Am I on camera? A Free apologizing to a 'Cycler for something? That never happens! I wish I was recording this because no one is ever going to believe me!"

"Shut up," Ellie tried not to smile. "I was just going to say I'm sorry you're such a loser." But they both knew she didn't mean it.

Ilya

Ilya squatted near the pool of dried blood and Ellie's bloody, discarded rifle. He studied the partial paw print pushing in the earth around the edge of the blood. Whatever made a paw print that size was no wolf. Not unless they had Arcwolves out here that weighed over four hundred kilos. And, from the stance, measured well over two meters from the flank to the chest. No, this was a monster, something out of the stories his father had forced him to listen to when he was very young. The hair on the back of Ilya's neck prickled, and he savagely stifled an urge to run back to the safety of the line like a terrified little boy. Tonight he knew his father would be laughing in his nightmares, ordering some great beast to pursue little Ilya across the endless muddy fields of sha sector.

Ellie and Abe's trail out from the border wall was easy enough to follow. Ellie's boots were barely noticeable, but that 'Cycler boy's steel bottomed boots tore up the ground and the boy seemed determined to break every plant in sight. Ilya had soon come to the old hunting enclosure and the blood. He skirted around the battle scene and followed the footsteps away until his Geiger counter told him the radiation was too intense. If they'd been out there this long in that radiation, they wouldn't be worth rescuing. Then Ilya had retraced his steps to the enclosure and gone over the bent grass and blood to figure out what had happened.

For whatever reason, Ellie and Abe had gone off course. Probably thought they could sneak off together and…it was best not to think about it for his blood pressure's sake. They'd gotten as far as the hunting enclosure before the Arcwolves attacked. Then Ellie had fought off the Arcwolves until this monster came. It had definitely consumed an Arcwolf at the edge of the clearing. Ellie must have seen its appearance as their chance to make a run for it. But either she or Abe got attacked.

Given that Ellie's rifle was left behind, she'd probably been fighting an Arcwolf and the monster had interrupted. So all that dried blood was from Ellie. There was no way Fat Abe could best a creature that size. The two of them had run off, Ellie wounded, into a high radiation zone. Ilya could definitely see Abe's tracks. The other set was too faint, but it showed Ellie's expert ability to move from root to root without leaving a clear trail. Even wounded, she was still holding to her training. Ilya felt his gut twist as his memory of holding his golden-haired girl tight to his chest flashed brightly. He grunted as he hurled the memory from him, down into the pit of worthless emotions a sector commander had no time to feel. He breathed deep, swallowed his emotion, and concentrated on the task at hand.

The monster had blocked them from returning to the border wall. It had forced them to run into the high radiation zone, but they didn't know that. Fat Abe had left his Geiger counter and oversized backpack in the enclosure. They must have been terrified. Whatever had savaged that backpack for food bars had cracked the enclosure door frame getting in and out. Tufts of grey and black hair were caught in the crack.

Ilya calculated the odds. Judging by the amount of blood she'd already leaked, Ellie was a goner. After a couple of days of high radiation, so was Abe. Maybe Abe was still alive out there. Ilya thought a little about going after him. But the boy would just come back to vomit his guts out and die in the radiation ward. No point in risking a rescue party out here with a monster loose. For what? To chase a good as dead 'Cycler boy and recover his daughter's corpse? It was probably a blessing that the monster had likely killed and eaten them both by now.

Ilya thought about how best to sell this news to Gladys. Best to say Ellie got surrounded and cut off by Arcwolves. She died protecting Abe. Both of them were monster meat by this point.

Ilya picked up Ellie's rifle and smeared it through the dried blood. It didn't stick, so he poured a little water from his canteen and let it dissolve the blood before he rolled Ellie's rifle in the mix. There, that looked permanent enough. A fitting tribute to his lost daughter. He rocked back on his heels while he let the blood dry on the rifle.

What had Ellie been thinking, falling for a dirty 'Cycler kid? From the size of Abe's destroyed pack, they were clearly running away together. But the rations would have soon run out. Then what? Subsist on Skullron crap and whatever stunted vegetables the Wilds provided? Make a homestead out here where their forbidden love could flourish? Ilya shook his head. Who could understand women? Especially if they fell for a fat 'Cycler instead of a real man like Todd.

Ilya blamed Gladys for letting them play together as kids. Fat Abe had infected his daughter with 'Cycler thinking and this was the result. Catastrophe and death. That's why Frees should stay with Frees and 'Cyclers with 'Cyclers. No mixing. Separate but equal. Well, not equal, because the 'Cyclers had their boots on the Frees' necks for as long as Ilya could remember. But separate.

None of that mattered now. His daughter's shame died with her. She'd died a Free hero guarding her charge. The rest would be forgotten as a bad rumor, unfitting to be repeated about a Free hero.

Ilya dragged the pack out of the enclosure and threw what was left of it on the ground. Let the Arcwolves and Skullrons scavenge it, turn it into nests and scatter pieces all over the area. It would make the attack site all the more believable if anyone else ever came this way. But that wasn't going to happen.

Ilya planned to let his report to Central of the monster leak. Ellie had been battling a monster, not just Arcwolves. It would raise her memory up to legendary status while scaring off any future expeditions into the Wilds. They'd all focus on the wall, holding the line against the monsters.

As he hiked back, Ilya wondered if he could convince Todd to say a few words at the memorial. Fine man, Todd, likely to be a leader on the line someday. No reason he couldn't be Ilya's replacement as commander of the sha sector, the son Gladys had never given him.

12 HEALING

Abe

"Owww! Son of a Skullron that hurts!" Ellie was complaining about Abe's exercising her limbs. Uncle Gabriel had been very clear that the null suit material was actively growing. It would continue to knit more tightly into Ellie's muscles. Lying around had already caused a small tear in her artery patch so that Ellie had started bruising and oozing blood down her leg. Abe had made it worse by assuming it was her time of the month until Ellie had told him she had a patch for that. "Frees bleed when you shoot them, not any other time, unless we're breeding." She'd explained it like Abe should have known better.

Uncle Gabriel had repaired the tear in the artery. During the procedure Ellie had refused numbing agents and chewed on a piece of a glove instead. Abe had been impressed, especially as just looking at Ellie's bleeding leg made him woozy. Her blood did have a sparking quality to it now. Not enough to spark like the Arcwolves, but enough to make it look like Ellie had swallowed silver filings.

After the second surgery, Uncle Gabriel had ordered Abe to stretch Ellie every couple of hours to keep the null suit flexible. It basically meant Abe got sworn at every couple of hours. But now, after a couple of days, Ellie had gotten used to the stretching. She still whined, but her complaints were more half-hearted, just enough to make sure Abe didn't think she at all enjoyed him twisting her around.

For Abe's part, he did enjoy it. Part of it was learning about the flexibility and the expansion capacity of Uncle Gabriel's null suit material. It felt like metal fiber, but it gave more like a synthetic cloth fiber. Not as much as an exercise stretch fiber, but somewhere in between the two.

And, yes, part of it was handling Ellie, who reminded Abe of something dangerous and wild, like a captured Arcwolf. Once she snapped at him, really tried to bite his hand, as he tried to stretch her neck. Only her hurt neck had slowed her enough to miss him. So Abe handled her cautiously, soothingly, never making eye contact, never threatening. He used all the techniques his mom Sophie had written about for working with wolves in the Beforer times, though Abe make sure he never told Ellie anything about treating her like an animal. Over time he was rewarded with Ellie relaxing more under his hands. She wasn't tame by any stretch of the imagination. But she did learn to tolerate his presence. It was better than Abe could ever have hoped for if they'd stayed on the line.

Ellie was healing, but she'd never be the same. Uncle Gabriel had injected her with more null suit bacteria as well as another bag of Arcwolf blood. When Abe had run one of Uncle Gabriel's Geiger counters over Ellie after the infusion while she was sleeping, she had sent it into a frenzy of beeping that nearly woke her. So Abe made sure to never handle her without his null suit and gloves and kept his helmet down when he was close to her.

As Ellie healed the Geiger counter level dropped to background radiation and even below. She started having night sweats and chills. Uncle Gabriel watched her for a day, then told Abe to suit up. "F-full suit, little Abe. Breathing a-a-apparatus too. Where we go not s-safe for you."

Ellie protested being woken up and moved. So Uncle Gabriel used one of his few remaining sedatives to knock her out. Then he and Abe carried Ellie in turns deeper into the Wilds. Abe was getting stronger, or Ellie was getting lighter, he wasn't sure which. But he was able to carry her for longer stretches. Uncle Gabriel also seemed much weaker than he had been. "I n-need this too," he explained to Abe. "Like a s-spa day for me."

Abe considered asking about the Arcwolves, but then he saw Scar sliding through the brush near the trail. The great Arcwolf was keeping pace with them, scouting ahead and checking behind as they moved.

They made it to a cave hole heavily overgrown by plants. "D-damn plants l-love this place," Uncle Gabriel pushed and cut his way forward. Several of the vines fought back, wrapping his knife-hand. Uncle Gabriel grasped the vines tightly with his other bare hand, inhaling deeply. The vines writhed away from him as if they'd been burned. "N-not like my n-nano-bacteria," Uncle Gabriel explained to Abe. "It takes their r-radiation."

As they went deeper into the tunnel, Abe started feeling his null suit heat up. It was like he'd put different parts of it next to a heating unit.

They came out onto a ledge, a few inches above a murky pool. Phosphorescing fungi lit up the water with a faint bluish glow, showing great roots stretching down into the water or lapping its surface like huge silent elephant trunks.

"P-put her in," Uncle Gabriel pointed to the water. Abe gently slid Ellie into the water. Even though he could feel the heat coming off the water, Ellie shivered as the water closed over her body. Only her head rested on the edge of the pool. Her body arched slightly, then relaxed.

Uncle Gabriel lowered himself into the water. The flowers that grew from his stomach injury, which had been wilting, began looking better immediately. "Y-you need to w-wait on the s-surface," Uncle Gabriel told Abe. "G-give us two- three hours. Too much isn't good. M-makes us t-too hot. O-overloads us l-like the suits."

"Is that why my suit is hot and vibrating?" asked Abe.

"Y-yes. Go r-run off some p-power."

Abe left them in the pool. Once he stopped carrying Ellie he realized he didn't feel tired at all. He felt amazing. Though Uncle Gabriel was joking, Abe did run back up the tunnel. Instead of getting tired, he got more energetic as he ran. All along the suit, wherever it touched his skin, there was a tingling, pricking sensation. It wasn't unpleasant, but the more it pricked the faster Abe ran. He burst out of the tunnel, scattering a pack of Skullrons that had been feeding in the clearing. Abe kept going, racing through the trees. He whooped and even grabbed onto a long twisting vine to swing on it. The vine writhed, but Abe felt like it was trying to twist away from him rather than grasp him tighter.

After what seemed like hours, Abe started to get tired. He hadn't been worried about the Arcwolves because he had seen Scar keeping pace with him a couple of times through the brush. Some part of Abe's brain led him in a wide circle back to the cave entrance. He found the tunnel and plunged back in, pushing the vines aside.

Uncle Gabriel had pulled himself out of the water. He looked up and smiled at Abe.

"Sh-she's awake."

Abe looked down at Ellie, who was looking up at him with a calm, dreamy wonder.

"G-get her out," Uncle Gabriel gestured to Ellie. "She's about c-cooked."

Abe reached down and hauled Ellie out of the pool. As he did so, his right hand started to burn. Cradling Ellie with his left, Abe looked at the null suit glove on his right hand. The null suit glove had split from where he had gripped the vine, and angry welts were already visible on his palm.

"R-radiation poisoning," said Uncle Gabriel. "C-cut off the hand before it s-spreads!" He pulled a saw-toothed knife from his pack.

Abe looked in shock at the knife and felt Ellie's hands close around his hurt palm. Before he could do anything, Ellie was kissing his palm. Not just kissing it, licking the wound. Abe stared at Uncle Gabriel as Ellie continued.

Uncle Gabriel shrugged. "M-might work. L-like sucking out sn-snake poison." He got up and Abe saw a bounce in his step that hadn't been there for days.

Abe hoisted Ellie on his back, but she resisted, holding onto his hand like it was her favorite toy. Uncle Gabriel led the way out of the cave, followed by Abe. Abe was amazed at how easily Ellie walked, keeping his hand close so that he pulled Ellie along by his hand.

All the way back through the Wilds Ellie kept her face on Abe's hand. She could walk as fast as he could. Abe wanted to ask Uncle Gabriel how the pool worked. But Ellie was too distracting. When she wasn't kissing his hand, she was nuzzling it. Abe found it a little unnerving, because he was enjoying her attention too much. He didn't trust it because he wasn't sure Ellie might not suddenly remember who she was and how she felt about him and bite off his fingers. But he had to admit whatever she was doing felt really good for his hand.

Even when they went back down through sets of sealing doors, the stairs, and into the lab, Ellie stayed on Abe's hand. He prepared food and ate one-handed, then fed Ellie bites while she played with his hand. Uncle Gabriel only examined the hand once and grunted. Abe could see that the welts were almost gone. Ellie refused to be parted from him. That night Abe had to sleep next to Ellie, who held his hand pressed to her face.

Ellie

Ellie had the strangest dream. She was part of a huge system of roots. She was a root, sucking the life from the water. The water was full of life, and she was drawing that life into herself.

With a sudden heave, Ellie was separated from the water. She felt abandoned and alone. Where had the life gone?

Then a dark hand was full of life. Life growing visible on the hand. She felt herself separated from life but the life continued within the hand. Ellie felt afraid and alone separated from the life. So she clung to the hand. It gave her life as she kissed it. The hand made her feel less alone.

Ellie woke up with Fat Abe's sweaty hand on her face. It smelled just like him, with his musky 'Cycler sweat. But that was also mixed in with stinking swamp water. Ellie shoved Abe's hand off her face and kicked him where he lay beside her. That would teach him a lesson.

"Ow!" said Abe, "What did you do that for?"

"Keep your smelly hands to yourself!" Ellie turned away from him.

"Guess you're feeling better," Abe turned away from her.

Ellie started to drift off to sleep again. But something Abe said bugged her. She was feeling better, feeling ready for line duty again. But she had been sick...Ellie couldn't remember the sickness. Everything before this moment was a blur, a dream. She couldn't remember where she was or why she was here.

Why was Abe sleeping next to her? Ellie had a sick feeling. Maybe Papa had really married her off to a 'Cycler like he'd threatened when she was young and disobedient. That was horrible! But maybe it could have been worse. There were a lot of 'Cyclers worse than Abe.

Ellie's mind drifted and she yawned. But part of her mind wouldn't let it go. If she'd been married off to a 'Cycler why didn't she remember the wedding ceremony? Shouldn't there have been a ceremony? Even Papa would insist on a Free ceremony with the traditional exchange of guns and ammunition. Ellie had set her sights on a pearl-handled .38 with exploding shells ever since she'd first thought about boys. She'd even mentioned it to Todd more than once when they'd gone to the shooting range together.

Todd! Wasn't she in trouble with Todd because Papa thought she was sleeping with Abe? He was right. Here she was sleeping next to Abe. So she was a floozy. Was she?

Ellie checked her memory, but it was still a blur. She decided they were clearly outside of wedlock because she'd never gotten her .38. She'd remember getting her .38, she was sure of it. How had she let herself be seduced so easily?

Ellie turned over to stare hard at Abe's back. He was sleeping with his arm thrown over his stupid face. "You could have at least gotten me the .38 I wanted, you cheap 'Cycler jerk!" Ellie shoved him.

Abe slowly turned toward her, "Wha…?"

"Don't give me that!" Ellie poked him. "If you're gonna date a Free, you should at least keep her in firearms. A girl deserves her weapon of choice. Even a 'Cycler should know that."

Abe blinked at her. "We're dating?"

Ellie's eyes narrowed. "Well, I certainly hope so. What is this to you, some casual get-together? You figured once Todd threw me away I was free for the taking? Well, I've got more self-esteem than that, mister. You'd best be budgeting for a nice pearl-handled .38, because I don't play around like this with anyone. You've got this Free girl now, so you'd best pay for me properly, put a gun in my holster, and keep us both honest!"

"Ellie, we're not dating," Abe tried again.

"Listen, you pathetic, immoral, 'Cycler scum," Ellie poked him and noticed her arm was covered in scars. It looked terrible, like something had tried to rip her arm off. "When did I tear up my arm?"

Abe yawned. "When the Arcwolf tore up your leg."

Ellie looked down at her leg. She had on a ragged pair of shorts made of the material of her border uniform, but they'd been shredded up to her thigh. Her leg looked like someone had gotten drunk and chopped at it with an ax. "Goddess love a gun! That looks terrible! It's amazing I didn't have that cut off. That's a killing wound, that is. I should have bled out in minutes." Ellie touched her leg.

"Why am I alive? I kind of remember an attack. It was really fast and the

Arcwolf had me. Shook me by my leg. I was dead. I blacked out and it was all over. Why am I not dead?"

"Do we have to do this now?" Abe yawned again. "If you're done sucking the radiation out of my hand, I can go sleep on the other side of the lab."

"What?" Ellie grabbed Abe's hand. "Oh, you're joking. Your hand looks fine."

Abe stared blearily at his hand. "It does. Thanks for that!" He yawned again. "I'll go sleep over there."

"Wait," Ellie felt really alone. 'Where are we? What happened? Are we dating openly or is it still a secret? Does Papa know? How come he hasn't killed you yet? Did you have a shootout with him and somehow win?"

Abe stood up and swayed a little. He screwed up his face in concentration. "Uncle Gabriel's lab, you were hurt, no and no, Not dating. Nothing to know, and no shoot out. I think that's it. Now I'm going to go back to sleep." He turned and walked to the far corner of the lab.

Ellie went to follow him, but she bounded up so quickly she took herself by surprise. She ran right into Abe's back and he stumbled to his knees. But before he could fall Ellie had scooped him up off the floor and was cradling him like a baby in his shiny null suit with its cute little hood.

"Wow!" Ellie tossed Abe up a little into the air and caught him. "Did you lose weight?"

"No, it's Uncle Gabriel's radiation tech. Makes you really strong. It's like if you had a constant adrenaline rush. Can you stop doing that?"

"Radiation tech? What do you mean?" Ellie was rocking Abe back and forth like a baby.

"I don't really understand it. Please stop." Abe had gone limp in Ellie's arms, which made him heavier, but only slightly.

"Well, I feel great," said Ellie. "I feel like I could run the entire line and back."

"You c-could," it was Uncle Gabriel coming in with a stack of boxes. "Our e-energy is un-unlimited for a short t-time. It l-lasts until the r-radiation runs down. H-half life decomposition."

"Radiation?" Elle saw the gut-shot old man with a weird flower growing out of his wound. "How are you still alive? It looks like someone blew your guts out your back. You should be dead, or at least crippled."

"Y-you're right," Gabriel stroked the flower growing from his middle. "Too bad your pa gut shot me and I f-fell into radioactive swamp water before he tried for the finishing head sh-shot. Put off his aim some."

"Papa gutshot you? Why?" Ellie still couldn't believe the old man was walking. From the side he looked like he was constantly sucking in his gut, and she could see where the headshot had torn away his hair in patches next to his ruined eye.

"Y-your ma," Gabriel sighed, "your m-ma was in love with m-me, and your pa is a s-sore loser. I took him with me to s-scout the Arcwolf packs. Sh-should have smelled a r-rat when he v-v-volunteered."

"Papa would never do that," Ellie jutted out her chin. "No Free would shoot an unarmed man. It's against our Code."

"D-don't you know all's fair in l-love and war?" Gabriel grinned like a wolf. "Y-your ma wanted me, and your pa w-wanted her. So he t-took me out. Got your m-ma and got you. But now y-you're m-mine."

"What?" Abe swung down out of Ellie's arms. He seemed more awake.

"Sh-she needs r-radiation to live n-now," Gabriel pointed at Ellie. "Th-that means sh-she has to live in the W-wilds with me. You d-don't think I saved Ilya's brat for h-him, do you? Sh-she's mine."

"You never said anything about that," said Abe.

"Y-you never asked," Gabriel shrugged.

"Could you have saved her without the radiation?" Abe looked at Ellie.

"M-maybe," Gabriel shrugged again. "No arm or leg. L-leave her a c-cripple. I thought about it. H-hurts him more this way."

Ellie looked at them both, then down at the floor. "You're both wrong. Papa doesn't care about me one way or the other."

Gabriel shook his finger at her. "M-maybe not. But your m-ma does. And your pa will do a-anything for her. So he'll come looking for you. W-when he does, I'll b-be waiting."

"You'd really use Ellie as bait?" Abe was standing between Ellie and Gabriel.

"S-sure. Didn't need to. G-got a plan to g-go over the w-wall and take out the w-whole s-sector. But faster to take out the l-leader first."

"Take out the whole sector? What are you saying?" Abe crossed his arms.

"L-look at her," Gabriel pointed a finger at Ellie. "Her kind and our k-kind can't exist together." He pointed to Ellie's injuries. "Her k-kind only understand k-killing. They're n-nothing but animals. I've b-been thinking about it f-for a l-long time. B-best to just w-wipe them out."

"You're talking about all the Frees? That's terrible!" Abe stared at his uncle.

"W-why? If they c-could, they'd w-wipe us out. A-ask her." Gabriel pointed at Ellie.

Ellie suddenly couldn't look at Abe. "It's true. Papa's talked about it with the other sector commanders for years. Getting rid of the employees, living on our own. But first we need Frees to learn how to run the thermal power plants. That's why Papa agreed to the integrated border school. If Frees can learn what 'Cyclers know we make you unnecessary. Then if you all disappear we keep Dubsee Central happy with no work stoppages. They don't care about 'Cyclers or Frees, just energy production."

Abe turned on her. "So all that time the Free cadets were learning circuits from me, with me helping them, they were planning to kill me?"

"Don't be stupid," Ellie flexed her new, improved arm. "They don't personally want to kill you. Well, maybe a few of them do. Actually, a lot of us thought about it when you would blow out our testing curve with your stupid perfect scores plus extra credit. But the older Frees just want to make you unnecessary and replace you."

"But what happens to the 'Cyclers if we're not necessary?" Abe was wide awake now and pretty angry.

"Well," Ellie shrugged. "'Cyclers don't like guns. It's not a fair fight, but that's not our fault."

"So you'd shoot me?" Abe was facing Ellie.

Ellie had to suck on her lip and think. She blew out her breath. "Well, I was gonna, but…" She looked down at her leg. "It looks like you saved my life. I can't shoot somebody I owe a blood debt. Maybe we'll call it even."

"Wait, you were really planning to shoot me, weren't you? It wasn't just an angry impulse, you planned it out with your pa? Shoved me out of the cage, planned to wound me, and then let the Arcwolves take me apart? Just like your pa did to Uncle Gabriel? And now you think we're even because you didn't manage to kill me and I saved your life? Wow. No wonder you suck at math."

"I-I told you," Gabriel smiled his crooked smile. "They're n-nothing but animals. I only saved this one b-because her p-pa will track her here. I w-want to s-see his face when he s-sees his f-freak daughter."

"Do whatever you want," Abe had his back to Ellie. "I'm sorry now we didn't leave her out there to die." He stomped off to the far end of the room and threw himself down on a stack of null suits.

Ellie wanted to follow him. But he was right. Her math didn't add up. Abe had done right by her, and all she'd done was do him wrong. It stuck in her throat like a chunk of dry food.

"Don't bother t-trying to figure 'C-cyclers out," Gabriel smiled at Ellie in the dim light. "I wouldn't expect your k-kind to understand k-kindness. Just remember, I m-made you and I can b-break you. So don't mess with m-me if you want to s-stay alive." He turned and left the workspace.

Ellie sat down. The energetic jitters still ran through her body, but she felt too heavy to move. It was one thing to be disgraced, to not meet Papa's idea of a perfect daughter. It was another thing to be a bad person. By her own standards, Ellie had become a bad person. Luring Abe out with a false promise to help him when she planned to gut shoot him and leave him for dead. Who did something like that? A snake in the grass, Papa would say. But if Gabriel was telling the truth, Papa had done the same to him. If Papa was a snake in the grass, what did that make her? Was she just the fool daughter of a liar? Was everything she'd been brought up on a lie?

13 SILENCE

Abe

Abe didn't talk to Ellie the next day or the one after that. He got food for himself and Gabriel, setting Ellie's bowl just inside the door of what had become her room. Gabriel had selected plants that he would drain of radiation, or that he would give Ellie in big bunches so she could feed her need for radiation before Gabriel turned them over to Abe in the kitchen to make soups and stews. Abe refused to ask her for anything.

Gabriel had Abe learning how to replicate his null suits. Replacing parts from existing materials was easy, but Abe wanted to understand the process from the null suits' origin through manufacture and creation. He found the whole process was straightforward, with the one reversal that radiation helped with culture growth rather than causing bacterial die-off. But the origin was always using Arcwolf blood.

Abe questioned Gabriel about creating a synthetic version of the Arcwolf cells. Gabriel showed him recent failed trials and dozens of past records. "N-nothing keeps them alive and in g-good sh-shape like l-living in an Arcwolf. S-second generation a-always dies." He shook his finger at Abe. "L-lucky for us, we've g-got lots of Arcwolves." Gabriel showed Abe a map of their part of the Wilds. "The r-red dots are packs. F-figure g-give or take five in a pack. S-sometimes as many as t-twenty. Some p-places I don't know b-because of the b-bears. A l-lot of strange a-animals out here. Th-think there was a zoo. S-scar keeps me safe. B-but don't g-go out without him. If the r-radiation don't k-kill you, the animals m-might. The plants feed the Skullrons, Th-the S-Skullrons breed like crazy and f-feed the Arcwolves. The A-arcwolves also eat the p-plants. It works b-but we're not n-needed in the s-system. You and m-me, we're just a s-snack."

Snack or not, Gabriel ordered Abe to make friends with Scar. Gabriel introduced him gradually, telling Abe he'd been bringing his scent up to Scar every day since he first arrived. Abe had to leave Cyrano in his room because even Scar saw all Skullron as scurrying food.

By the time Abe had the courage to enter Scar's personal den, he was covered in sweat. Images of Ellie's attack by the huge Arcwolf kept playing through his head, and Abe had to stifle the urge to run off and wash his hands. He slid inside the door flap of Scar's den and stood absolutely still. Abe's breathing sounded like a bellows in his ears. He tried to make himself quieter, but then started holding his breath and wondered if he would pass out. Abe had to lean forward and put his hands on his knees to keep from falling over.

Even though it felt to Abe like he was making a racket, Scar barely acknowledged him. The great wolf barely glanced up from chewing a knotted burr out of his tail hair. Abe took a single step forward, and Scar kept chewing. Another step, and the great wolf yawned, showing a disturbing number of glistening teeth. Abe stopped, feeling his armpits drip sweat. Scar stared up at him, then rolled himself onto his feet and circled Abe. Abe stood and didn't move until Scar shoved at Gabe's hand with his head. Abe didn't know what was expected, but his hand automatically went to scratching behind the great ear. Scar leaned into Abe's hand, almost pushing Abe over. A few more scratches and Abe was shoved back until he sat down suddenly. Scar followed Abe down, resting his great head in Abe's lap.

After that first meeting, Abe was always welcome. Scar discovered Abe was a sucker for rubbing him behind his ears as long as he wanted. The Arcwolves had various mites that thrived on the Arcwolf blood and the residual electrical charge. If they got really annoying, Scar would scatter them with a violent bout of electrical static and by shaking his body so hard it looked like he was trying to turn his body inside out. But they'd hop back on as soon as he calmed down. It was so much easier for Scar to flop down his immense head onto Abe's lap and let the fully null suited and grounded Abe scratch behind his ears. Officially for Gabriel Abe was conducting his own research about the diversity and interspecies mating of the Arcwolf mite populations, but really it was just an excuse to scratch behind Scar's ears until long after Abe's legs had fallen asleep under the weight of the great Arcwolf's head. There was often a lot of drool involved, Scar's lips flopping open in pleasure so that he appeared to be grinning up at Abe.

It was Scar who brought Abe to see and to get to know the rest of his pack. One day he got up and grunted for Abe. Gabriel had just taken a sample of Scar's blood. He told Abe, "S-scar w-wants you to f-follow him. I'd go, b-but be careful." Abe walked behind the Arcwolf through the null suit flaps of what had to be the biggest doggie door he'd ever seen.

On the other side, down an unlit tunnel, was a cave filled with Arcwolves.

They turned as one when Scar came in. Abe found himself surrounded. He could barely breathe. The Arcwolves answered Scar's huffed call and padded over in twos and threes to sniff and snuffle at Abe in his null suit. Despite his comfort with Scar, Abe had a sense of dread that he might be a new chew toy for the pack. The last Arcwolf to come over was a great wolf who touched noses with Scar before giving Abe a perfunctory sniff. Abe had the feeling she'd be much happier if he had been a meal for the pack. But several of the young Arcwolves broke the tension at that moment by showing up with some kind of horned beast with too many legs carried in between them. Scar nudged Abe back toward the doggie door before padding off to join the rest of his pack in feeding.

After that, Abe was welcomed by the pack. Well, he was tolerated at least. Some of the pack adopted him as the pack ear scratcher. The rest ignored him or growled at him if he got too close. Except for the big female, who purposefully bumped into Abe or growled at him whenever Scar wasn't around.

Abe didn't mind. He'd figured out that the pup Ellie had shot must have been the big wolf's pup. Several other females would come and lie with her, and occasionally she'd nuzzle an empty patch of earth next to her as if it once had contained another body. Abe even considered what it would be like to lead Ellie out into the cave and let the big Arcwolf finish what she'd started. But even at his angriest, Abe couldn't see a time when he'd be able to do something like that. How had Ellie been able to be so cold about planning to kill him? How could it be so easy to kill? Abe found himself wanting to ask her despite himself.

Ellie

The walls were closing in. It was a very big room, Ellie kept telling herself. A really big room. And it wasn't like she was completely alone. Gabriel came through occasionally, taking a sample of her blood, leaving her piles of radioactive plants, and giving her things to do. Granted, they were things like, "M-move all these boxes over th-there," or "Hold st-still while I w-work on you, or "G-get stronger." But it was at least semi-human interaction. Ellie had taken "get stronger" to heart. In the last few weeks, she'd gotten stronger than she'd ever been in her life. Her floor exercise routines had moved from two to one-armed. Now she was using individual fingers to lift her weight.

But every morning the walls were closer in and Ellie had a harder time catching her breath. Now it had gotten so bad all Ellie could do was sit with her knees up to her chest, arms wrapped tight around them, head down. Strangely, that seemed to help. As long as Ellie held that position, the walls didn't close in as much. She had a vague memory of being locked in a cupboard so small she couldn't lift her head. It was so tight she couldn't move, so she focused on just breathing. Just breathe, she told herself now, and someone will come for me.

When Ellie had asked Gabriel if she could go outside, he'd just stared at her. Ellie guessed what he was worried about. "I won't tell anyone where you are," she started. Gabriel shook his head at her and smiled. "N-no, you w-won't. N-not until I'm r-ready."

The only thing that helped Ellie with the walls besides huddling in a ball was when Abe brought her food. In the silence, with the background hum of the instruments and the far-off sound of dripping water, Ellie could hear Abe's reluctant footsteps far off down the hall. Abe always got softer when he got closer to her door, like he was trying to be sneaky or trying not to wake her. As if he didn't sound like someone slamming a rifle butt on the floor all the way down the hall. It made Ellie laugh every time. Big dumb 'Cycler boots were more metal than synthetic leather. They studded the bottoms for longer wear, which made them about as stealthy as a gunshot.

Abe would always stop outside the sliding door. Ellie supposed he was listening and wondered if she should make snoring noises or some kind of racket to put him at ease. But once she'd tried it Abe just stood outside longer until she stopped. Then Abe would slide open the door just a tiny amount, slide her food in, and close the door. He'd pick up her used bowl where she'd left it outside the door. Then he'd forget about being sneaky and go clumping back down the hall, sounding like a spilled bucket of ammo until his noise finally quieted.

When Ellie first heard Abe coming she could breathe. It lasted until she finished her food and put her hard fiber bowl outside. The room didn't even seem as small. So she started taking longer and longer with her meals, gulping the last mouthful only when she heard Abe coming back again. As long as Ellie could keep the memory of Abe going, she was fine.

But the benefit of the meals was fading now. Ellie couldn't feel her breath for more than a few minutes after Abe left. She tried to keep up the illusion, even stomping around her room like Abe in the hopes of keeping the sound of him around would keep the walls back.

It wasn't working, and Ellie felt herself suffocating even with her knees drawn up and her chin down. She needed to get out and she realized that the door had never been locked. Only Ellie was keeping herself in this self-imposed prison out of guilt. Guilt about what she'd done to Abe.

As soon as she realized she could leave, Ellie started following Abe down the hall. Where he was noisy, Ellie was cat silent. She found every hiding place and followed Abe along at his pace while leaping from walls to ceiling and back. Ellie stayed above or on the side of Abe as he worked in the workshop or in the kitchen. He never noticed, and when Gabriel caught her lurking he just sniffed and left her in her hiding place. Cyrano, Abe's pet Skullron, would watch her silently from Abe's shoulder but never alerted Abe to her presence.

So Ellie had the run of the bunker. She could breathe as long as Abe was nearby. Her breathing only stopped when Abe went out into the Arcwolves' cave.

Ellie could smell the Arcwolf rooms. Her sense of smell had gotten painfully acute. They smelled dangerous. Elle had once crept silently into Scar's room toward the outer doors leading to the outside. The Arcwolf had been waiting for her, staring straight at her as she crept across the ceiling. As she tried to cross the threshold into his room he growled. It was a barely audible sound, but it had all the finality of death. Ellie had no doubt that Scar would kill her instantly if she trespassed into his area. So she waited, hidden, knees to chest, arms wrapped tightly, head down until Abe returned from the Arcwolf den. Cyrano would sneak out of Abe's room and sit in the shadows a safe distance from Ellie to watch with her. They waited in silence together.

One day Abe didn't stop at his workstation like he usually did. He clomped off down the hall toward Ellie's room. She followed him, curious. It wasn't her mealtime. He was going to check on her? Why?

Abe knocked on Ellie's door and waited. Ellie hung from the ceiling, concealed between two pipes. What now? She couldn't think of a way to get around Abe without terrifying him. Maybe she could knock him out, then go past him and open the door. Ellie decided against it, but only partially because it was mean and a terrible idea. The other reason was that Ellie didn't trust her own strength anymore. She knew how much force she'd needed before to knock someone out when she trained in fighting at the border wall, but now she could climb around like a Skullron, effortlessly holding up her own weight. What if she struck him too hard and killed Abe instead of knocking him out?

The idea made Ellie's breath catch. Without Abe, she couldn't breathe. He was her only link to the wall, the sky, the two milers stretching farther up than you could even see. If anything happened to Abe, Ellie wasn't sure she could ever breathe again.

Cyrano had scampered up onto Abe's shoulder as he walked along the hall. Abe had long since given up trying to keep the Skullron in his room. Now the Skullron stared silently up at Ellie. Flicking his little tail, he raced down Abe's coveralls and scratched at Ellie's door. Abe looked down at Cyrano and slid open Ellie's door. "Ellie?" He walked into the darkened room. Ellie climbed through the door after him, keeping to the ceiling over Abe's head. Cyrano had raced to the far side of the room and was making a lot of unnecessary noise.

"Ellie!" Abe had wandered to the far side of the room.

"What. I'm right here." Ellie dropped to the ground and tried to make herself sound bored.

"Yikes!" Abe turned. "I've got to get my eyes checked. I didn't even see you! Sorry to bother you, but I've been trying to understand how to get tough enough to be able to kill someone. Gabriel says there are no 'Cycler programs I could use to learn. Is there some sort of Free training I could do?"

"Why? You plan to kill me?" Ellie made her voice flat. Abe would be within his rights. Any reasonable Free would have attempted it by now. Ellie could take him, but she wondered if she would. Maybe she'd let him kill her rather than defend herself. Without him, she wouldn't be able to breathe.

"Honestly…" Abe looked away in the dim light, "I was thinking about killing you a little bit. But I can't bring myself to really consider it, much less carry it out. I think there's something wrong with me. All the Arcwolves can kill without hesitation. You had no problem trying to kill me. So I'm the one missing something. I'd better fix it because there's no place in the Wilds for…"

"For a coward?" Ellie cut him off. "Forget it. It doesn't take courage to kill. Trust me, Frees are as scared as anyone. You just have to be more scared of what that Arcwolf will do to you if you don't shoot him. But a lot of Frees still miss their shots. If you don't lock your arms in place, your body will jerk away at the last second. It's not natural to kill."

"But you can do it…" Abe wasn't looking at her.

"Are you saying because I'm a girl I shouldn't be able to kill? Something in my tender female nature should stop me? You looking to get punched?" Ellie advanced. She had been down this road so many times with so many Free boys. It usually ended with them on the ground bleeding, Occasionally she had to dislocate something to make her point.

"No!" Abe ducked. "I want you to teach me how to kill."

"You want me to teach you how to kill so you can kill me? Do I look that stupid?"

"No, I'm not going to kill you," Abe threw up his hands. "I probably should, but every time I think about it I get sick in my gut. Why? Are you still planning to kill me?"

"No! I need you!" Ellie felt and heard the terror in her voice before she could control it. She tried to fake her way out by shrugging. "I need you to make my food and run my errands. All my servant stuff."

Abe nodded. "I'm useful. Fine. If we're not going to kill each other, will you teach me how to kill? I want to be able to go up into the Wilds without dying. Gabriel says he's ready to test his improved null suit. I'm the first chance he's had to use it on someone who can't handle radiation. So I'll be the first person in the world to use the suit that might change 'Cycler society forever. I got poisoned by radiation before, but that was because of a tear in the old suit and full radioactive water immersion. Gabriel wants me to try longer periods with the intact new suit to see if I develop radiation poisoning."

"Wait, he's sending you up? Outside? Is he crazy?" Ellie felt her chest tightening at the thought. Abe would be going away, no telling how long. "What happens if you get radiation poisoning?"

Abe blushed. "I wouldn't expect you to do…what you did before. Gabriel would be able to fix it, I think. But it's not going to happen because Gabriel's null suit design is pure genius! He's created a secondary shunt system that redistributes radiation throughout the suit. So if you have one radiation hot spot the load is sent all over the suit. The hotter the spot, the faster the passive circulation goes."

"But that means the whole suit gets radiation," Ellie couldn't control her agitation. "If it cooks you, you'll be completely dead. Full body burns."

Abe nodded. "It's a possibility. But a remote one."

"No!" Ellie stamped her foot. "It's too dangerous. You can't go."

"Of course it's dangerous," Abe got his I-know-everything voice. "All experiments can be dangerous. But if we're successful, it means that the 'Cyclers can move freely into the Wilds. We could even colonize the deepest areas. It would be a dream come true! 'Cyclers could be completely free of Dubsee. We could live independent of any oversight, living on the resources of the Wilds."

"What about 'You can't go' don't you understand?" Ellie had her hands on her hips now.

"What about scientific exploration don't you understand?" Abe wasn't backing down for once in his life. This was his chance to really be a hero.

"Fine. If it's so important, I'll do it." Ellie sighed.

"You can't, because your body likes radiation. You can't even come with me because you'll throw off the test because you absorb radiation. I'm the only one who can get radiation poisoning."

"Exactly. So you're the only one who can't go. Your uncle could hook me up with some kind of monitor."

Abe thought. "No, that won't work. The radiation messes with electronics and the Wilds are lousy with fluctuations. We couldn't trust the readings. So the only real test is human blood."

"But not your blood. We'll find someone else." Ellie wasn't going to let this happen to Abe.

"Why not my blood? Why not me? Am I not good enough to be a hero, is that what you're saying?" Abe could believe he was listening to this Free girl who'd always put him down. "I don't need to listen to you, because nobody made you my mother. So I'm going, whether you like it or not. So are you going to teach me how to kill things, or not?"

Ellie wanted to punch him, knock him out, and tie him up. That way he wasn't going anywhere, ever. But she knew he wouldn't appreciate what she was doing for him even if she was saving his stupid life. Abe had that committed look in his eye. It was a look she'd seen in Todd, and it was a look

Papa got every day when he was done talking about something. So Ellie sighed and nodded.

"Fine. I'll teach you. Defend yourself." She threw a ridiculously slow punch at Abe's head. He stuttered and flailed until she connected. Then he went limp and fell to the ground.

"Perfect," Ellie stood over Abe. "Perfectly wrong. If you want to die, that's how you do it. If you want to kill, do the opposite. Now get up and we'll try again."

It took twenty tries before Abe could even block. Twenty more before he could block effectively. He was maddeningly slow, but he could learn. Ellie called it a day when Abe started fumbling from fatigue.

"Practice," she told him. "We'll start early tomorrow after breakfast."

Ellie had to admire Abe's work ethic. He clearly practiced. She silently watched him practice hour after hour while she sat with Cyrano perched near the ceiling in a dark corner of his practice room. By the third day, he could block anything she threw at him. Even when Ellie used her enhanced speed, Abe watched her shift weight and saw her coming before she threw her punch or kick.

Attacking was another matter. After another week Abe stayed miserable at attacking no matter how much he practiced. Ellie tried to motivate him with anger or fear, but Abe wasn't motivated by either. At last, Ellie threw up her hands, "I give up."

Abe put his hands on his knees, breathing hard. "I've..been..thinking about this problem. Ask me..ask me if..it's relevant to the..task at hand."

"Relevant to..what?"

"Relevant to the task at hand," Abe straightened. "Just keep asking me that."

"Is it relevant to the task at hand?" Ellie was just trying it out and wasn't expecting the speed of Abe's blow. She barely blocked.

"Wow! OK." Ellie shook her head. "Weird 'Cycler trigger for aggression. But fine. Is it relevant to the task at hand?" This time Abe tried a two-part attack that Ellie barely dodged. Twenty minutes later they were both covered in sweat, but Abe seemed ready to keep going.

"All right," Ellie rolled her shoulders. If she was tired Abe must be in agony. "Let's move on to weapons. Since most of what you meet out there will be armed with claws and teeth, we should prep you for those attacks."

Ellie picked up a long piece of piping, striking low at Abe's legs and feet. She was training him to knock away something coming in low. Then they practiced blocking and stabbing punches to get out of the way of some larger creature. Abe started getting clumsy from fatigue, but Ellie kept him at it. She told herself that whatever was attacking him wouldn't give him a break because he was tired.

It was one thing to teach Abe when he could think about it, and another thing entirely for him to do it without thinking. All Ellie had to do was shout or distract him, and Abe's fighting skills would fall apart.

Abe started doing radiation exposure testing of the new null suit in the lab with Gabriel long before Ellie felt he had any chance above ground. Abe still had a bad habit of slumping if he got overwhelmed. It wasn't a full collapse like it had been, but he'd go into a defensive-only mode that irritated Ellie. "Sometimes you have to kill to survive, Abe! It's relevant to the task at hand!"

Ellie knew Abe would never be really ready. She'd spent her life fighting and he'd only been at it for weeks. But Ellie also knew Abe would hit his breaking point soon. She'd seen it so many times with Papa. Papa would blow up and go do something even if he wasn't ready. It was what her mom called "man crazy." Ellie had learned to get ahead of it. So she told Abe after one long practice that tomorrow he'd be ready.

"Really?" Abe was surprised. "What did I do different today that makes you think I'm ready?"

Ellie shrugged. "Nothing. I just figured you're about ready to go anyway. So I thought I'd give you permission."

Abe laughed. "You're right."

They looked at each other, both smiling. Ellie saw Abe start to reach out to her, just a little twitch of his hand. Then a cloud crossed his face and he turned away. Ellie fought the urge to reach out to him. It wouldn't be fair. He'd already been hurt too much by her. She had no right to expect anything from him.

14 OUTSIDE

Abe

Tomorrow Abe would go into the radiation zone with the new null suit. He couldn't sleep. Abe kept trying to remember everything that Ellie had taught him. Half a dozen times he got up to go ask her to show him a move again and then lay back down because he knew that would be crazy. If he didn't know it by now, he wouldn't get it by trying to cram it into his brain.

At dawn, Abe got up. Gabriel was already up, puttering around his new null suit to put a few last-minute changes on for Abe. "D-don't worry. I-I'll send Scar with you. It's f-for just a f-few hours. H-he'll let y-you know if something's c-coming. D-don't want anything t-to wreck my s-suit the first d-day out."

"Thanks." Abe wasn't sure if Gabriel was joking. At times he was sure his uncle cared about him. Other times it seemed like Gabriel thought of him as a lab experiment. Abe suited up, feeling the null suit's layers encase him. The little microfibers were stripped off one of the plants out in the Wilds. Gabriel had figured out the fibers sucked radiation up like a straw. Well, not exactly. More like a biochemical cascade that redistributed the radioactive particles throughout the plant. But it had the same effect of taking radiation away from the skin.

Once the radiation was wicked up, Gabriel's flushing system pumped it all over the suit where the Arcwolves' nanobacteria converted it to food, growing the next generation of bacteria and rendering the radiation harmless. If it worked perfectly, Abe should be able to withstand almost any amount of radiation. But only if it worked perfectly. Gabriel said he hadn't had it melt on him, which wasn't the most reassuring of tests. So Abe was the first real test. He'd be famous if radiation didn't kill him and he wasn't eaten by something in the process of testing it.

Abe checked all his overlapping flaps. The suit went on in one piece to minimize any problems with flow from one part of the suit to another But it zipped in the back and Gabriel had installed flaps along the closure to wick away any radiation buildup on Abe's back. Adjusting the face mask was tricky as well. It had been fitted to Abe's face, but he needed to wear a radiation-shunting gas mask to prevent inhaled radiation from building up in his lungs.

Gabriel fussed over Abe, inspecting him and stepping back again and again. He poked disapprovingly at the loose bunching around Abe's middle. "Sh-shouldn't be l-loose. Did you l-lose weight?" Abe started to apologize, but Gabriel waved him to silence. "N-no matter. Better to t-test a suit with a l-little slack. G-go up now. Scar is w-waiting."

Abe came up blinking into the grey sunlight. How long had it been? It had to have been weeks and weeks, maybe months since he and Gabriel had taken Ellie to the radiation pools. Gabriel had gone back on his own but he hadn't wanted Ellie to leave the lab after she found out she was bait. Instead, Gabriel had brought back buckets of the swamp water for Ellie to drain of the radiation as well as the plants from the higher radiation zones. So Abe had been down there with her all this time.

Scar slid out of the brush, brushed against Abe before stopping and sniffing the air, and then led the way deeper into the Wilds.

Ilya

Ilya was sweating even though he knew it wasn't hot. He wiped the sweat from his forehead and stared at it. Was it raining? He was drenched. How long had he been out here? No matter.

It wasn't good for morale to leave a lineman's body for the Arcwolves, Ilya told himself. He needed to keep up his men's morale. Franklin's new radiation suit also needed testing. The suit was garbage, but it let Ilya justify all the radiation exposure he was getting as he slowly circled out from his daughter's original attack site.

All the rest of the sector commanders knew by now that Ilya spent every spare moment hacking his way through the brush of the Wilds looking for the remains of his daughter. He was doing it to bring her back and give her a proper hero's burial. It would help the morale of the line, since they all had just gotten turned down for any pay increases once again by Central. Central hadn't even bothered to respond to their requests or appeals. No communication whatsoever. The Frees didn't even get an official no. That meant fewer recruits, not that they ever had any that Ilya remembered. The Frees could use a hero's burial to bring up spirits. Even if it killed Ilya to bring her back.

There was definitely one reason Ilya wasn't out here in the Wilds, whacking away at the plants that fought back. It was definitely not because

Gladys had moved out all her things and was living above the pantry now. Gladys hadn't spoken to him since Ilya had come back with Ellie's blood-covered rifle and his story about his daughter's heroic passing. The rest of his sector and the line had accepted his story, but Gladys had seen through the partial truth. She'd holed up with Sophie, and the two of them had scoured scratchy, fuzzy security recordings.

One of the security tapes had a mirrored window image of Ellie kicking the hell out of Todd and two of his buddies. When Sophie showed him the footage, Ilya had pretended it could have been anyone, or at least any woman destroying Todd. But he and Gladys both knew how fast Ellie could move. Only Ellie could have taken down Todd and two other che linesmen that fast.

It was Ilya's refusal to question Todd about his activities on the day that Ellie and Abe disappeared that had been the final straw for Gladys. She told Ilya point-blank that he cared more for "that muscled idiot" than his own daughter. Gladys had it in her head that Todd and his buddies had hunted down Abe and Ellie after Ellie bested them. Sure, the Arcwolves were involved, but only to clean up after Todd and his two friends had already killed Abe and Ellie.

Ilya had hoped it would blow over, but it hadn't. So he was living alone, eating all his meals in the cafeteria even though Gladys had promised to love, honor, and obey him in sickness and in health. Wasn't losing a child a kind of sickness? Shouldn't they be supporting each other rather than arguing over whether Todd was involved?

Ilya couldn't bear it if his protege, his replacement, had been involved in the death of his daughter. Who else could take command of the sha sector? When Ilya brought back Ellie's wolf-eaten body, Gladys would see he was right. All this unpleasantness would be behind them. But if Todd had been involved…Ilya put the thought away. He would find her body. It would give him the peace he needed.

At first, Ilya had tried to follow the great beast's tracks. They were easy to follow, but they led in nearly a straight line back into the deepest parts of the Wilds. The creature must roam all of the territory inside the wall. Ilya figured it wouldn't have carried Abe and Ellie's bodies off. It would have left them behind as it had the well-chewed carcass of the Arcwolf pup.

So Ilya had returned to the original site. Circling the first attack site hadn't paid off yet, but Ilya was hopeful. The Arcwolves were efficient. They wouldn't have dragged the bodies very far. Finding the bones would show it was the wolves, not bullets, that had ended Ellie and Abe. Ilya didn't want to think about what it would mean if Abe or Ellie's skulls showed bullet wounds. Of course, he'd argue they were self-inflicted. Some kind of lovers' suicide pact. But it would be too suspicious. He'd have to question Todd and do what was necessary to bring justice to the line. Ilya would have to challenge

Todd, duel the one boy he hoped could replace him as sector commander. He'd have to put his own needs as a Free father above the needs of the sector. It was an impossible situation.

Even with his mind wandering, Ilya couldn't miss the new tracks. They were fresh and clumsy. These weren't the tracks of any Wilds monster, not unless it walked on two legs and wore...Ilya crouched down..yes, there were the telltale treads of a null suit!

The short hairs on the back of Ilya's neck prickled. What was someone else in a null suit doing so deep in the Wilds? He briefly had a vision of his old enemy Gabriel, face twisted in pain, as he clutched at his null suit. What if something foul had taken over Gabriel's body and was still powering his corpse through the brush? What if the dark man of Ilya's nightmares really walked the Wilds? Ilya tried to laugh at himself, but the sound came out hollow and strangely flat inside Franklin's cheap face mask. Ilya gripped his rifle tighter. If it was Gabriel's dead body it was still a body. And whatever had a body could be killed. If he found Gabriel's body out for a walk, he would take it down. Ilya would then make sure it was cut into pieces and buried in separate graves this time. He stalked after the fresh prints. It wasn't the bodies of the kids, but if Gabriel wasn't staying dead maybe Ellie and Abe weren't either. Maybe that was why Ilya hadn't been able to find them.

Abe

Scar took Abe deep into the Wilds. The Geiger counter was beeping so much Abe turned it off. He checked the suit for heat, but it only felt warm. After maybe an hour Scar sniffed Abe over and turned them around. Another half-hour and Scar stopped suddenly, sniffing the air.

Abe came up to the great Arcwolf and started to speak. He liked talking to Scar because Scar was a great listener and never talked back. Abe also talked to Cyrano, but he'd had to leave the little Skullron behind in the lab. Gabriel said the Skullron could throw off the suit's readings. So Scar was Abe's second choice for a conversation partner.

But now Scar huffed at him and Abe fell silent. They stood without moving for what seemed like an hour before Abe heard a stealthy noise off in the distance. Scar faded back into the brush before disappearing. Abe considered moving, but realized any effort he might make at concealment would likely be so loud as to bring whatever it was on top of him. Abe's best chance lay in confronting whatever it was and hoping that Scar would get behind it and catch it by surprise. So he stood his ground, a statue in his glistening null suit.

Another hour seemed to pass. Abe listened intensely, but all he heard was the wind through the leaves. Insect sounds made Abe suddenly aware of how alive the Wilds were all around him.

Then Ilya stepped out of the green, his rifle leveled at Abe's head. Even Abe knew that wasn't the best and safest shot to take. It was much safer to do a body shot. That much had been driven into Abe at the integrated border school.

The other strange thing was that Ilya's rifle was shaking. Abe had never seen Ilya nervous, much less shaking. Abe had seen Ilya face down a crew of angry linemen threatening to string him up without so much as a flinch. Until this moment, Abe would have sworn Ilya didn't know how to even fake being nervous.

"G-Gabriel?" Ilya's voice sounded hoarse across the clearing. "You won, Gabriel. Gladys moved out. She isn't even speaking to me. Even dead, you won. Why are you back to haunt me?"

Abe couldn't think of anything to say, so he said nothing. Ilya took another step closer. "You look good, Gabriel. Your suit looks new. I figure you look so good you must be a spook. I'd gut shoot you again, but it wouldn't do any good, would it? It'd just go right through you because you're not real. The shot would bring every monster around here running. That's what you want, right? For me to die from your monsters just as you planned all those years ago?"

Abe stayed absolutely still. Ilya had the look of someone gone wrong, someone who'd been exposed to too much radiation. The part of Abe that kept track of such things even in a crisis measured how warm his suit was and what that meant for radiation exposure. It wasn't bad, so Ilya must have gotten his exposure somewhere else. Or maybe over time? How long had it been? Abe tried to calculate the time passage while he worked on keeping his breathing shallow and calm.

Ilya had decided Abe was Gabriel and was telling him why it was his fault he'd been shot. "You wouldn't stop, you wouldn't leave her alone. It was me she was supposed to be with, and you wouldn't listen. Crazy 'Cycler! Don't you know it's unnatural for 'Cyclers and Free to be together? You wouldn't breed an Arcwolf and a Skullron, would you? Gladys was too much woman for you. She's too much woman for even me. Why do you think I'm out here, you damn fool? I'm here looking for the bones of my dead daughter. Gladys has broken me, made me her idiot thrashing about in these damn mutated weeds. Unless I find my daughter, I can never go home again."

At that moment Ellie, scarred and tattered, crouching like an Arcwolf, stepped out of the brush between Abe and Ilya.

15 HUNTED

Ellie

Following Abe silently through the brush had been the easy part. Ellie had avoided coming too close to Scar, who had tolerated her. But when she got too close, Scar let her know to stay back by stopping and looking back at her with his lip curled.

Leaving the lab hadn't been easy. Ellie didn't know the way, but Cyrano seemed to. The little Skullron had been pestering her since Abe left. Ellie had ignored it until Cyrano nipped her and she'd followed him more out of anger than an urge to get out. Gabriel kept all the doors oiled, and Ellie had slid them open and closed behind her without noise. But the only way out led through Scar's den. Ellie's courage failed her, but Cyrano dashed into the Arcwolf's den without pausing. She'd had to creep through Scar's domain to get to the outside doors, and all the time she climbed along the roof toward freedom she kept looking to her right, to the great Arcwolf door that led out to the den. If any of the other Arcwolves smelled her, she would be trapped and killed.

The hardest part of leaving was realizing that if any of the Arcwolves out hunting from Scar's pack caught her scent they would hunt her down. So Ellie had taken to the trees after Cyrano. Some of the trees weren't happy to house her and slapped at her with rough, slow-moving branches. She kept above the ground the whole time and would have never been able to stay up with Scar, who slid through the forest like a great, shaggy Skullron. But Abe was a turtle. Ellie found herself exploring to the sides out of boredom, wandering back and forth across Abe's path while Cyrano kept watch over him. His plodding never wavered, but never sped up either. Ellie got the sense that Scar was resisting the urge to lie down and nap while Abe caught up. Several times the Arcwolf sat on his haunches and yawned, pawing at his long face with the almost human expression of, "Why me?"

Ellie had been off exploring, looking down at an old settlement overrun by vines and immense flowers, when Cyrano had run to her and nipped her. She hurried back toward Gabe. Ilya's voice reached her first, a rumbling tone cutting through the buzzing and rustling of the Wilds. Ellie eased her way closer, listening to Ilya's voice. His voice trembled and wavered, very unlike his usual precise, cutting tone.

When Ellie came out of the brush and saw Ilya for the first time she almost gasped. Ilya looked sick, he shook slightly, and his eyes had the wild, chased look of the radiation ward. Ilya hadn't seen her yet. He was busy babbling about Gabriel and ma. Ellie had a hard time believing that gentle Gladys, her calm and smiling mother, would ever have stood up to Ilya the way he described. Something terrible must have happened for even ma to turn against him.

But those thoughts were in the background. The important thing was to talk Ilya down, to get him to stand down and not shoot Abe. To not shoot Ellie's medicine that kept her sane down in the depths of the underground lab.

Ellie stepped between Abe and Papa. She was ready to spring at Ilya if she must.

Ilya

"Ah," Ilya gestured to the specter of Ellie, torn and scarred, that seemed to appear out of nowhere. "Here you are, the ghost of my dead daughter. Are you going to lead me to your bones? No? No matter, I'll find them eventually. After all, the Arcwolves can't have crushed them all." He gestured around at the brush. "Any idea where I should start looking?" Ellie silently pointed him back the way Ilya had come. "Back behind me? Probably. I've been doing circles out from the attack point. But I could have easily overlooked some hollow in this damn jungle."

Ilya turned. He had the feeling of something unfinished. He turned back. "You look good, Ellie. Death suits you." Ilya stared at the silent ghost of his daughter. "I expect we'll see each other again soon. I've been getting burned from the inside." He tapped his head. "Baking me slowly. Not a good end for a sector commander. I wish I could go out in a blazing battle. Maybe take that old hound Scar with me." Ilya turned to go, and Scar stepped out of the brush to block his path.

The great beast was obviously part of his radiation haze. Ilya wasn't scared. "Scar, old enemy. You won't get my bones to gnaw on. Not like my Papa or his Papa before him. I know it was you who ambushed them both, out here. No, I'll spend my last days whining and vomiting in the radiation ward." He approached the great muzzle, hand outstretched.

Scar sniffed, retreating before Ilya. "Don't you want to finish me? Spare me the pain?" Ilya lowered his rifle and pulled down his null suit, baring his throat. "Here you go, fresh meat. Take your best shot." He laughed, a wild sound that flattened into silence against the enclosing trees. Scar turned tail and slid back into the brush.

Ilya was seized by a fury. "My blood not good enough for you? Come back and face me, you coward. Come back and kill me like a man." He lunged into the bushes, crashing after Scar. The Arcwolf vision was gone. But a tiny Skullron, one that seemed vaguely familiar, ran just ahead of Ilya, leading him farther and farther into the Wilds. Only when it disappeared did Ilya try to retrace his steps. When Ilya finally thrashed his way back, the ghosts of Ellie and Gabriel were gone as well. He stared about him at the tiny clearing. Something troubled him about Gabriel's ghost. But Ilya felt the heat in his head and headed back to the line. Only after lying in bed for several hours that night could Ilya remember what troubled him. The grass was trampled. He'd been following something that left footprints. "Ghosts don't leave footprints, do they?" Ilya asked the empty room, the piles of his discarded clothing lying in heaps with old mess kits and enough disposable toiletries to give a 'Cycler a heart attack. "What the hell was out there in Gabriel's body?"

Abe

"Stop pulling me!" Abe hissed at Ellie.

"Shut up!" She hissed back. "If he hears you he'll shoot us both just to see if we're ghosts."

"I think he's long gone now," said Abe. "Did you notice he was shaking? I'd swear he's got serious radiation poisoning. But my suit wasn't heating up, so he's gotten it somewhere else."

"He's been searching for my body," Ellie felt a lump in her throat. "Mama must have sent him out to find me. Papa won't give up searching until he finds me or dies trying." She felt a wave of regret wash over her. "I should have told him I was real, gone back with him."

"Are you crazy?" Abe gripped her arm with his null suit glove. "He was so close to shooting us both. Even Scar ran away from him. He's so mad with radiation sickness even the Arcwolves won't touch him now. Gabriel said that was one of the reasons Scar and his pack didn't eat him when they had him and he was gut shot. Animals sick with radiation taste bad. Like too-spicy food. The one thing that would save your dad now is if Gabriel injected him with Arcwolf blood."

"Papa would rather die."

"Looks like he'll get his wish."

"Don't say that." Ellie turned away.

"Sorry," Abe fiddled with his null suit gloves.

"No," Ellie was quiet. "He'll never do anything medical. Papa figures he's better off cutting off his own leg 'cause he can do a better job. He'd never turn himself over to the 'Cycler quacks in the health wing."

"Seems like typical Free stubbornness." Abe tried to stop himself, but it was out.

"Sounds like typical 'Cycler arrogance. You think there's only one way to live and die. Don't forget a dumb Free just saved you from getting shot."

"Shot by another Free who's so stubborn he won't get treated for radiation."

"Papa's made his bed. He'll lie in it soon enough."

Abe could see Ellie fighting tears. He racked his brain to change the subject. "How'd you find me?"

"Your pet Skullron showed me. Plus you make a bigger trail than a broken hovercar."

"What are you doing out here anyway?"

"Saving your dumb hide, evidently."

"You know what I mean. I don't think Gabriel wanted you outside at all. You'll throw off the experiment and he doesn't trust you not to go running off back to the line to blab about him to your father."

"You can tell him I didn't run off, I don't blab, and my Papa thinks I'm a spook. And that my Papa is dying of radiation sickness. So if your uncle Gabriel wants to take his revenge on Papa he'd better hurry up. I don't think Papa's got much time left."

They were interrupted by the appearance of Scar. He sniffed the air and trotted over to Abe, pushing Gabe's null suit with his nose. Scar trotted ahead back to the lab. Abe looked around for Ellie, but she'd disappeared.

Ellie

It was easy to pass Abe and Scar. Halfway back to the lab Ellie was joined by the darting little Skullron. Ellie was safely back in her room by the time Abe got back and de-suited. She thought about pretending she'd never left, but realized Gabriel probably had surveillance cameras that had recorded her leaving.

Abe came to see her as soon as he got back. "Gabriel heard about our meeting your dad. There's a microphone recorder on my suit that worked pretty well even in a radiation field. It transmitted back some of our conversations."

"Good to know," Ellie looked closely at his old, indoor null suit. "Are you recording us now?"

"I don't think so," Abe looked around. "But with cameras as small as they are, we can't know for sure without some kind of scan."

"Why are you here?" Ellie wanted to pretend the day hadn't happened, that she hadn't seen her Papa shaking from radiation sickness.

"Gabriel wants to know if you'll help lure your father out here to get treated. He thinks having your dad dependent on him for his life would be a great laugh. Well, he does now. I talked it up for the last hour. How having your dad stuck out here in the Wilds, forever kept away from Gladys, would be much worse than having him torn apart by Arcwolves."

"So you want me to be the bait?"

Abe looked serious. "Listen. We both know your dad is dying. He's bad enough that they can't save him even if he checked himself into the radiation ward. Once the brain is starting to cook, that's a very bad sign.

"The one chance he's got is with Gabriel. But he'll never volunteer to get treated. So taking him as a prisoner is the only way to save his life."

Ellie was quiet. "Why would you want to help him? All he's ever done is be mean to you."

"You still want to help him and he's been much meaner to you."

"Yeah, but I have to. I'm his…"

"Daughter that he never wanted? Anyone else would have been overjoyed to have a kid like you. You're smart, dedicated, extremely athletic, and the best shot of your class. You're most Free parents' dream. Only your dad would be constantly finding fault with you. He's the evilest parent I've ever seen. Right up to the time you shot Scar and he didn't believe you. As if you would ever fool around with a 'Cycler like me."

"You're not so bad. At least you've never shot someone for love."

"That's true," Abe smiled a little. "If that's how low your bar is, then even I meet it."

"But Papa and I don't."

"You've never gutshot someone..oh, you meant me. Forget about that for now. Will you help get your dad out here or not?"

"I guess." Ellie nodded. "At least we can try."

Abe

Once Ellie had agreed, Abe figured out Ilya's schedule. Ellie's dad wouldn't be out in the Wilds when he was still due to be on guard duty. Even in his radiation-addled state, Ilya would never miss his duty call. Both Ellie and Abe agreed on that, so it was just a matter of figuring Ilya's next day off. If he followed the proper rotation, it would be in three days.

The plan was simple. Ellie would meet her father and lead him out to the lab. He'd follow her, thinking she was a spook leading him to her bones. Outside the lab Abe would meet them, leading Ilya down into the lab where he could get treatment. Neither one of them spoke about what would happen to Ilya after he got better. Abe hoped Gabriel could be reasonable, seeing that having Ilya free to roam would be best for everyone. But he really wasn't sure. Gabriel was preparing for Ilya's coming with too much anticipation. He told Abe, "W-we don't have e-enough anesthesia. It's going to b-be quite p-painful." Abe saw his uncle's grin of satisfaction.

16 SHOT

Ellie

Ellie waited for Papa at the edge of the wall. Scar had taken her this far, growling if she got too close to him. Ellie still kept to the trees when she could, but they were stunted this close to the wall and had fewer leaves due to all the plant poisons the Frees kept spraying to keep the foliage off the wall. The number of Skullron also increased as she went, so that by the time Ellie reached the area of the wall she and Scar scattered packs of the huge-eyed creatures feeding as they passed through. For the first time, Ellie realized without the Arcwolves the Skullrons would overpopulate and spill through over the wall and into the world city. She knew the border wall line men threw down poison and traps. But clearly, it wasn't slowing the population on this side of the wall.

Ellie heard a single stone shift farther out. A clumsy footfall, one that would have gotten Ellie a lecture if she had done it. Papa was coming. Scar had faded back into the brush. Ellie wasn't sure if the Arcwolf was staying to watch or heading back to the lab.

Ilya was coming fast. He wasn't being cautious but still moved with the careful quiet of a veteran linesman.

When Ilya stepped beyond the last wall, Ellie stepped out to greet him. Ilya stopped. He clutched his head and rubbed his eyes. When Ellie didn't disappear, Ilya leveled his rifle at her.

"You are not real!"

With a sudden sureness, Ilya shot Ellie in the gut. The shot echoed off the wall as pain blossomed in her middle.

"Papa?" Ellie barely had time to whisper the word as she crumpled.

Ilya ran forward. "Ellie? Ellie! I thought you were some kind of creature or a delusion. But you're bleeding, really bleeding. Oh, I shot you. It's you, it's really you? Ellie, what's the Free code I taught you? Tell me so I know it's you. Oh, it can't be you. What's the code?"

Ellie looked up at him. "Live Free or die, Papa." Then she passed out.

It was a long time before Ellie could think clearly after that. She was in a bed in the radiation ward, white curtains pulled closed around her bed. Ellie was momentarily overwhelmed by the chorus of beeping machines and the sharp scent of antiseptic spray in the air. Two 'Cycler doctors whispering to each other in the corner of her room outside the curtains. Ellie heard snatches of what they were saying, "..healing like crazy..never seen..too radioactive to live..poisoned her father…" Ellie faded out again.

Ellie woke in the night ravenous. It was a hunger like nothing she'd ever known. Something was sucking her dry, taking away her soul. Ellie looked up at the forest of tubes and lines that snaked up from her body. First, she reached out and unplugged the blinking monitors that ringed her. Then she felt around and deliberately pulled each line free so that they dribbled on her blanket with multi-colored fluids. One of them was warm, and Ellie held the sack until it cooled in her hand. When the last one was detached, Ellie staggered to her feet. She didn't know what she was doing, but if she didn't eat, she would die. Of that she was sure.

Moving in a haze, Ellie slid open the door to her room. Down the hall to her left was a lighted desk with several bored medical staff chatting. Ellie thought about calling out, but somehow felt they didn't have the food she needed. Above them was a sign that read, "Radiation Ward: Exposure patches Required." Looking up, Ellie saw a sign above her door. "Terminal," it warned, "Use Full Precautions." Looking to her right, Ellie saw two more doors with signs like hers. She slid her way along the wall to the next door. Sliding open the door Ellie had the vague notion that this patient might have food. Anything that could quench her hunger. But the room was bare except for a bed enclosed in a tangle of lines and stands. As Ellie went closer she saw an elderly 'Cycler woman, her dreads laid out on the pillow around her head like she was surprised. She was asleep and breathing shallowly.

Something about the woman's bandaged hands called to Ellie. She reached down, grasping the woman's bony wrists. There was a trickle of something there, a taste of what Ellie craved. Ellie drank it to its last drop, then put her hands on the woman's bandaged body. The bandages slowed Ellie's drinking, so she wormed her way under them. The woman's skin felt dry and cool. But there was a warmth burning inside. Ellie sucked at the warmth, drawing it into herself. She was startled by a bandaged hand brushing her face. Ellie looked down and the old 'Cycler's eyes were open. "Thank you, honey. Whatever you're doing feels wonderful. The pain is much less now." The old woman's eyes fluttered and she slept again.

Ellie finished with the warmth. Her hunger was just as bad. She needed a lot more. In the next room, Ellie could almost feel the heat through the wall.

Back out in the hallway, Ellie peered cautiously back at the lighted station. The nurses hadn't moved. She slid along the wall, noting handholds available in the ceiling in case she needed them.

The next door had lots of warnings on it. Ellie ignored them and slid open the door. Inside she could smell him before she saw him. The mixture of tangy sweat, the acrid odor of gunpowder that clung to him, and the aftershave Papa always wore because his Papa had worn it. It was Papa in the tangle of tubes. Ellie slid into them, finding Papa's too-hot body.

Papa felt clammy. He was sweating, but his sweat smelled like the Wilds. Ellie could feel one of the machines Papa was hooked up to draining away the heat. It was storing it in a little pouch, and Ellie drained the pouch, ripping it open with eager hands. The machine was far too slow. The heat was in Papa's blood, in his brain, surrounding his heart. Papa was burning up. He would die, burned to cinders inside by all that lovely heat.

Ellie gripped Papa, sucked at his heat. Her body pulled the heat into her. She pushed her way onto Papa's bed and lay down next to him. The whole length of her body bathed in his lovely heat. Ellie fell asleep cradling Papa's head in both hands, warm and full at last.

17 REVENGE

Abe

Uncle Gabriel was angry. Abe had never seen him this angry. The anger made his uncle stutter so much he was coughing. But Abe understood well enough that Uncle Gabriel was very upset that Ellie hadn't returned with Ilya.

"B-b-betrayed!" Uncle Gabriel kept shouting. He'd periodically blame Abe for bringing Ellie, for keeping Ellie alive, and for not talking Gabriel out of sending her out as bait. "H-he'll b-be c-c-coming! With h-his st-stupid m-men! Sh-she'll l-l-lead'em r-right h-h-here!"

Uncle Gabriel was more than angry. He was setting his original plans into motion. The Arcwolves would attack the sha sector in a mass. They would overrun the sector and break free into World City Bela. While the sector was distracted, Uncle Gabriel would kill Ilya. Dubsee would retaliate by removing all the leaders of the Free, sending them to the asteroid belt as punishment for their failure to protect the city. Once new leaders were chosen, Uncle Gabriel would repeat the attack in a different sector. He estimated after a dozen attacks Dubsee. would deport all the remaining Frees and put employees in their place. The Frees would be gone for good. Nothing less than absolute destruction of their kind would satisfy his uncle.

Scar had been howling all evening, and different packs were howling back. Already several other packs had shown up and lolled in the pack den. Abe knew they wouldn't be there for long. Uncle Gabriel intended to have the packs overrun the sha sector before Ilya could get reinforcements. This many Arcwolves might not have posed a threat if the sector had been fully staffed and rebuilt. But the line had gone begging men for so long every linesman was desperately needed. Abe suspected Ilya's brutal treatment of his men had made their sector of the line one of sparsest. So even this crowd of mangy curs would make mincemeat out of the few linesmen arrayed against them.

The line would be overrun and the Arcwolves would escape into the world city.

But none of that seemed to trouble Uncle Gabriel. He was focused on the Arcwolves finding Ilya and killing him. So Uncle Gabriel kept pointing out Ilya's workstation and home apartment to the old wolf as if Scar could understand him.

Abe kept out of the way, but he knew he couldn't let this happen. As much as he hated the Frees, they didn't deserve to be wiped out.

Someone had to warn them, and Abe was the only person who could. He slipped away from Uncle Gabriel, which wasn't hard because Gabriel was shouting and raving incoherently now. Abe outfitted himself in Uncle Gabriel's new null suit and quietly slipped out of the lab. It was impossible to avoid Scar's territory, but the great arcwolf was busy elsewhere. Doing the best he could to avoid leaving tracks, Abe made his way toward where he had met Ilya. On the trail, Abe immediately was met by two of the younger arcwolves from Scar's pack. Instead of stopping him, they jostled Abe for ear rubs and growled at any strange arcwolves that sniffed at them from the brush. The two seemed happy to trot along with Abe, nipping and rolling one another, dashing ahead or behind to try and catch a stray skullron. They stayed with Abe all the way to the old shelter where he and Ellie and been attacked. It was just getting dark, but they'd made very good time. From the shelter, Abe could see the glow of the light from the border wall. The two young Arcwolves nuzzled Abe once more and then trotted off back into the Wilds as if they'd just been out hunting.

Once he made it to the lights of the wall, Abe was suddenly uncertain. Would Ellie even want to see him? If she'd rejoined her father, then Ellie would die of radiation hunger even as her father died of radiation poisoning. The Arcwolf mitochondria inside Ellie needed radiation to live. Abe might be coming back to a pair of funerals and likely a chain of beatings from the angry sha sector Free.

Abe took a deep breath through the null suit filter. Regardless of Ellie, he needed to warn the line that the Arcwolves were coming in force. They needed to get reinforcements or to get clear. He wondered about Scar. How smart was the old Arcwolf, and what did he gain from helping Uncle Gabriel? What did he gain from helping Abe escape?

Ellie

Ellie woke to a mix of noise. Several people were talking at once.

"I must insist…"

"Look at these readings!"

"Ms. Barnaby wants to be discharged…"

Ellie peered under one eyelid at the room. A nurse was chasing around two doctors with null suits over her arm. Another nurse was waving a clipboard at them. Both doctors were ignoring the nurses and staring at Papa's readouts. Papa! Ellie looked up at Papa.

Papa was looking down at her. When he spoke, his voice came out a raspy whisper. "I gut shot you, my malenki. Radiation cooked my head. I thought you were a spook from my nightmares coming to life. I Should have known my girl would pull through a wolf attack. Survival is in our blood. I got us both back here and checked myself into this quack ward. This is the punishment I deserve for not believing in you. I figure I'm too far gone for them to do much for me besides watch me die."

Ellie squeezed his hand. It was the nearest thing to approval and an apology she'd heard from him since she was small.

"Where's my Ellie?" Gladys had come into the room. "She's not in her room. Is she dead? Did I miss her? Oh, she's with you, Ilya."

Ilya stared at his wife. "Are you talking to me now?"

"I never stopped talking to you, you idiot. I just couldn't bear you putting that thick-headed Todd over our own girl. But you did good. You brought our girl back. I told you she'd been shot out there. Probably by that no-good boy or one of his buddies. It's a miracle she survived out there this long. Doctors said she should've died a long time ago." Gladys hugged them both through the tangle of tubes.

"I feel really good," said Ilya after a minute. "Doc, whatever you're doing I feel great. Maybe your treatments do work."

One of the doctors looked up from the screens. "You should. The radiation in your blood is down below the background levels. We're not sure how..."

"It's called a tough constitution, son. I'm from old country stock," Ilya told him. "If I'm clean, can you clear off all these tubes? I've got a line to run."

In less time than Ellie thought possible, she was walking out of the radiation ward with both her parents. Her gunshot wound was mostly healed, and the doctors said the bullet had been almost near the surface, like her body had been working it out for some time. No one believed the shot was recent, so that was her and Papa's secret. He was happy to let Gladys think she'd been right all along. It was better than explaining how he'd shot her daughter in a radiation haze. They would deal with Todd later when they had to come clean. But for now, it was better to let things be good for once.

Gladys said it was time to bring Ellie home to fully heal. Ilya could "Come along if he wanted to." It was the closest thing to forgiveness that Gladys could manage on short notice. They all knew it was contingent on Ilya confronting Todd and his cronies about ambushing Ellie out on patrol. But it could wait for a bit while Ellie healed.

Abe

It was strange approaching the line with fear. Abe had lived his life on the line. He knew many of the towers and the great tangles of barbed wire so well he could draw them. Here was the wire cyclone. Over there was the crumbling jawline of the giant he'd imagined had died and formed the original wall. But after so many weeks away, after so much time with Gabriel, Abe felt shy and nervous about coming back to a place that had so long been his home.

Cyrano, who had been snug inside the null suit, noticed that he wasn't moving. The little Skullron burrowed his way up to the face mask and chittered to be let out. Abe took him out carefully, setting him down on the ground rather than risk damaging the suit. Cyrano took off for the line, tail held high. Abe found himself following.

The linemen watched Abe closely as he walked to the outer gate. He found in surprise that it had been left open, held only by wire hooks. Abe guessed Ilya had done away with the key system once he started going so often into the Wilds. So Abe didn't have to stop until he got to the final gate, which was still locked and reinforced. Abe rattled the gate for the linemen who stood fifty paces away. Cyrano had already pushed under the gate and disappeared.

"Identify yourself," one of the linemen stepped forward.

"Abe King, thermal coupling apprentice," Abe gave his official title.

"Fat Abe?" The other linesman walked toward Abe. Abe recognized him as a classmate, Jeff, from border school. Jeff couldn't be much older than Abe, but he was pulling full line duty already.

"Yep," Abe unfastened his mask and grinned at Jeff.

"Wow," Jeff took the gate key from his companion and went to unlock the gate. "Never figured we'd see you alive again. Rumor was that Todd ended you out there in the Wilds months ago. But Commander Patton did bring your girlfriend in a couple of days ago."

"Ellie?" Abe felt his breath quicken.

"Yeah," Jeff's face darkened. "She was in a bad way. Somebody gutshot her a while back. The rumor is that she beat the pants off Todd and his buddies outside mess. You know anything about that?" He didn't wait for Abe to answer. "Gonna be hell to pay if it was Todd. Linesmen don't ambush their own." He glanced at Abe's null suit. "You look good. The suit must have worked for you. How'd you two live out there so long?"

Abe was trying to think how to answer and Jeff held up his hand. "Never mind. I don't want to know if it involved Skullron poop soup. You can take it up with the commander at your court-martial."

"Where is Ilya?" Abe remembered the urgency of what he had to do.

Jeff's face was troubled. "Checked himself into the radiation ward. Left his deputy, that bookworm Jacob, in charge. We're all hoping it was a precaution, but the commander's been acting a little...chaotic lately. Got us all up at three a.m. to march around just to show the Arcies we weren't afraid of them. Crazy stuff like that."

"Hey," said Jeff's companion, a grizzled linesman named Ed long past retirement age, "don't talk sass about the commander. He'll be fine."

Jeff hung his head. "Sorry, sir."

"Thanks for letting me in," said Abe. "Hey, uh, watch out for Arcwolves, OK?"

"Always do, always do," Jeff saluted him. Abe realized the Free boy had taken his words the same way he might if someone had said, "Be safe out there." Abe wondered how he could make the threat more real without sounding crazy. But he didn't have time to say anything, because his mother Sophie was running over the broken pavement of the courtyard to grab him and hold him so tight that Abe could barely breathe.

18 HOME?

Ellie

Ellie tried not to notice how empty the little apartment was without her Mama's things. Discolored patches on the walls showed where pictures had been hung for years, now packed away in boxes and stored above the sha sector pantry.

They were all trying to have an early dinner and pretend none of it had ever happened. Ilya complimented Glady's cooking, saying he hadn't eaten this well in weeks and then falling silent. Gladys watched Ellie like a hawk, refilling her plate multiple times until Ellie protested.

"Mama, I really can't eat anymore."

"Of course, you can. What on earth did you eat out there?"

Ellie paused. "Well, mostly Skullron soup."

Gladys pursed her lips and ladled more food onto Ellie's plate. "My point exactly. Besides, as far as I know, you're eating for two."

"Mama! What? I was gut-shot. There's no chance…"

Gladys shook her head. "Shot didn't hit your female organs. I asked. Getting shot doesn't mean your 'Cycler…'"

"Abe's not like that, Mama," Ellie said it with a finality that paused both Gladys and Ilya's eating.

"So where do things stand between the two of you?" Gladys asked. "I know your papa is dying to know, but he's got no right to ask because he didn't do what a Freeman should have done and confronted Todd. But I'm asking. Is Abe going to be buying you that pearl-handled .38 you've been pining after forever since you got your first .22 rifle?"

Ellie looked down at her plate. "I don't think so. I don't think he's coming back at all." She felt her chest tighten like she couldn't breathe.

"Do you want him to?" Gladys was merciless.

Ellie colored, but said nothing. She could feel her parents glance at each other over her head.

"Listen, Ellie," Ilya weighed his words. "You know Abe wasn't my first choice. But if…"

"Don't start on me, Papa!" Ellie flared. "You've got no right after what you've done. Abe never laid a finger on me except to help me heal. He was nothing but a gentleman. I don't care what anyone says about 'Cyclers. He was more of a gentleman than you or I will ever be." She bit back more words. "May I be excused, please?"

Gladys nodded. "Go ahead. Your papa and I have things to discuss."

Ellie stood up. Her legs were shaking. She wanted to run and hide, to fight someone. Anything but think of never seeing Abe again, never hear the trudging thump of his dumb 'Cycler boots or the tinkling windchime of his toolbelt.

Abe

Abe stood in the cracked courtyard of the sha sector and let himself be hugged. Sophie hugged Abe long after Jeff and his companion had a chuckle at his expense and walked off on their rounds. She held him long after they were out of sight. Sophie held Abe as if he was an apparition and only by holding him could she keep him from drifting away like mist.

When Sophie finally stepped back from Abe she said in a perfectly calm voice. "You've lost weight. It looks good on you, that null suit. Fits you well. Reminds me of your uncle."

"Thanks, mom," Abe wasn't sure what else to say. "I'm sorry…"

"So," Sophie cut him off. "How is Gabriel?"

"How..how did you know?"

"I didn't. Now I do. When my son walks out of the Wilds after months still in one piece he had someone helping him besides that crazy Free girl. Especially if she was gut-shot the whole time. Add in a new null suit that looks like what Gabriel was working on when he disappeared. It's not hard to put the pieces together."

"Uncle Gabriel's good, but he's really angry."

"Understandable. I'd be too if Ilya left me for dead out there. Did he shoot Gabriel and leave him for dead? I've always suspected."

"Yes, he did. How did you figure…"

"Well, come on, son. We both know the Arcwolves better than anyone on this side of the border. They don't carry off one prey unless it's much weaker than another. Why deprive the pack of extra fresh meat? Maybe I'd have believed Ilya if he'd come back missing a leg. But he must have wounded Gabriel. There's no other reason a pack would have let him get away."

"You're right, they did. But now Uncle Gabriel is coming for Ilya. He's going to use…"

"He'll use Arcwolves he's trained to try and break our line. I've been watching them scouting the line for months. They know our patrol times to the second and jump over just after the patrols pass. But Gabriel is wrong about the Arcwolves obeying him. They have their own reasons for wanting to get across the border."

Abe looked at his mother.

"What?" Sophie stared back at him. "Everything you know about Scar and the Arcwolves I recorded and put in the sha sector database. When you were gone I kept myself sane by going over every search you did on that database looking for clues. You even left me notes about your suspicions on your workstation. A mourning mother is a fearsome researcher. I've been watching Scar's movements for years. He's almost human, patient and cunning."

"I wondered," Abe said. "Scar seems way too smart to just let himself be used."

"Magnificent creature," said Sophie, "and you're right, he's using Gabriel to distract us from the Arcwolves' real purpose. They'll come because they want to get past the line into the old sewer system. There's a whole hunting ground down under World City Bela that they used to get into through the underground thermal pipes. Ilya's grandfather collapsed their pipes one by one, and his father finished the job. That's why the Arcwolves broke through and went into the city before. They were trying to find a way down into their old hunting grounds. When they were cut off, I think the original pack was divided. The other Arcwolves have been trapped down there in the sewers all these years."

Sophie sighed. "Even though Gabriel's wrong about the Arcwolves, the chaos they'll cause will let him go after Ilya in the confusion. But their fight is nothing if the Arcwolves have to search the Dubsee streets for a way down. If we want to avoid the worst of it, we'd better make sure there's an easy, open route into the sewers behind the lines."

"Do you know all of this because of the security recordings?"

"No, I know all this because I've read all of the Arcwolf reports for the last hundred years. I've also read between the lines of those reports. Doesn't it seem strange to you that the news continues to report Arcwolf sightings in the sewers but there hasn't been an attack on a Dubsee employee in decades? The last attack was a sewer worker who surprised an Arcwolf mother and her cub down in a blocked pipe. He just got bit and lived to give lots of interviews about the terror of the Arcwolves" She paused. "God, it's good to see you! You look just like your father when you're thinking hard."

"How did you know about the coming Arcwolf attack?"

"I know because in the last few months since you disappeared -never do that again, you hear me? - there have been no sightings of Arcwolves anywhere along our line. But as soon as Ilya comes back with Ellie, there have been so many sightings they're putting two or three in every report. That tells me they're testing the line, organizing themselves into a giant pack. But the sector commanders won't listen to me.

"Ilya might, but he's been in the radiation ward. He just got discharged today. I was on my way to see him when my baby walked out of the Wilds like he's just been gone for an afternoon.

"Look at you! Do you see this grey hair? I didn't have this grey hair before you left. But now you're back with your shiny suit. At this point, half the line probably knows you're back. Not hard to spot that shiny suit, and only my son trudges like he's carrying the world on his shoulders." Sophie hugged Abe again.

Something squirmed at shoulder height inside Sophie's clothes. "Oh," Sophie reached inside her coverall. "I believe this is yours." She pulled out Cyrano. "Little fella ran right up to me and climbed my coveralls. I almost didn't recognize him after all these years. That's when I knew you had to be back and I came running." Cyrano squirmed his way back under Abe's null suit as Sophie hugged him again.

"We need to tell Ilya about the Arcwolves," Abe said at last.

"Are you sure you want to do that before you show your father that shiny suit he's been trying to make all these years?" Sophie fingered the suit.

"That's a tough choice," Abe said with a smile, "make dad jealous or save World City Bela from destruction."

"You know it's not that," said Sophie. "Your father has missed you terribly. He can hardly focus, keeps forgetting things. I've caught him staring at your picture. He hung it up next to Gabriel's in his workshop."

"But how am I relevant to the task at hand?" Abe couldn't keep the bitterness out of his voice.

"You know that's his way of trying not to get hurt," Sophie put her arm around Abe's elbow. "I've never been relevant to the task on hand, but we still had you. Don't let Franklin's BS get to you. He's a little boy who's been hurt badly by the world. Remember, Gabriel was his parents' favorite."

"All right," Abe relented. "We can see dad. But right afterward we warn Ilya that Uncle Gabriel is coming for him. A lot of people could die."

Abe and Sophie climbed the stairs to Franklin's workshop quietly. Abe could here his father muttering to himself inside. The door was open partway and Abe saw Franklin's back bent over a steaming vat of something that smelled like Abe's socks when they got lost under his bed. The workshop was sheer chaos now, no semblance of order anywhere. Abe was surprised at how small Franklin seemed to him now. When had dad gotten those gray hairs? Had he always slumped like that?

"Hey, dad," Abe found his throat was tight.

"Not now! Can't you see I'm busy?" Franklin shouted back. "It had better be relevant…Abe?" Franklin stopped and turned.

"Abe? Really Abe?" Franklin lifted his arms up. They were coated with thermal coupling lubricant and a black slime from acid rain corrosion. But Franklin's stumbling awkward hug was the best Abe could ever remember getting.

After a long moment, Franklin stepped back. "Let me look at you. My, you're taller. Were you always this tall and I didn't notice? We should measure you officially." Then Franklin noticed what Abe was wearing and his eyes glazed. "Is that a null suit? Of course! That's how you survived. What is it made of?"

Suddenly all of Franklin's attention was directed at the suit. Abe could feel the moment slipping away as his father rummaged in a pile for a measuring device.

"It's good to see you, dad. Good to be back. We can talk later, but right now I need to try and save lives."

"Could I just get a piece of the suit? Maybe a glove?" Franklin was lost in his curiosity. Abe hugged him again and then pushed Franklin away as he tried to remove Abe's hood. "I'll be back, I promise." He and Sophie left Franklin scribbling down notes and following them to try and get a reading off the null suit as they descended the stairs.

19 REUNITED

Ellie

Ellie had left the dining room table was walking down the hall to her room. She was fighting to breathe, fighting the weight on her chest that got heavier every time she thought about never seeing Abe again. The door chime sounded.

"Ellie, can you get that?" Ellie heard Ilya's habitual call. She wanted to scream back at him but stopped herself. Had he yelled it out for the months she wasn't here, letting his voice echo in the empty apartment? She imagined him rising only when he realized she wasn't here to do his bidding? She was about to stalk past the door when she felt a coolness beyond the door and smelled a hint of a tantalizing fragrance. It smelled like dirt, 'Cycler sweat, and the Wilds. It was the most amazing aroma she'd ever smelled. Ellie yanked open the door.

"Abe!" He was there, sweaty, shiny, and looking surprised. Ellie wrapped her arms around him before she thought about it. "You're here. You're really here." She pulled away when his suit got ice cold against her.

"I don't like your suit. It's cold." Ellie started to shiver.

"Oh," Abe looked down at his suit. "You're why it suddenly got so warm. Yeah, we need to talk about that. You need to get some radiation or you'll shut down. But right now I've got to tell your dad about…"

"Gabriel?" Ilya stood in the hallway. He had his personal engraved revolver in his hand but it hung loose and relaxed. "Are you Gabriel's little messenger come to tell me he's coming for me? That's one of his suits, isn't it? So he's still alive out there after all. I thought I was just seeing things."

"Still alive in spite of you," Abe couldn't keep silent.

Ilya nodded. His jaw worked, but he said nothing.

Gladys came up behind Ilya. "Maybe you should finally tell your side of the story, my milyi."

"Doesn't matter, what's done is done."

"It matters," said Gladys. "Show them why you missed. Show them what was done to you before you shot at the Arcwolf."

Ilya was silent. "A Free doesn't show weakness."

Gladys touched his arm. "It's not weak to show the truth."

Ilya shrugged. He pulled up the sleeves and slid the dress commander tunic he always wore over his head. Ellie realized she'd never seen papa without his long-sleeved tunic. Underneath Ilya's torso was raked with scars like he'd been dragged over razor wire. He held up his right arm, which was missing the bottom of the muscle in a jagged oval. Ilya smiled at Ellie. "I can't stretch out a couple of fingers, but I can still use my trigger finger and hold a gun." He pulled his tunic back on quickly. "Sorry for being disgusting. The only person who has to deal with it is your mama. I was lucky."

"So tell them how you were injured," Gladys prodded Ilya.

"What's to tell?" Ilya shrugged. "I shot Gabriel after he sicc'd his trained Arcwolf on me. He sprayed me with blood and knocked my rifle out of my hands. I guess he didn't figure I'd live long enough to get the gun back. When I did, the damn fool jumped between me and his precious wolf to protect it. I gut-shot him. He staggered off after his wolf and I took pity on him. I tried to finish him off rather than let him bleed to death or get torn to pieces by a pack out there. He went down into the swamp, but I guess I missed. If he's coming for me, it's no more than I deserve. I left him for dead."

"So you didn't shoot an unarmed man?" Ellie could feel some part of her relaxing inside, something deep down that she'd been holding tight.

Ilya furrowed his brow. "Well, he wasn't armed in the traditional way. Didn't have a weapon on him. That's the only reason I agreed to go out with him into the Wilds on his scouting trip. I figured I could take him in a fair fight. We were going to settle our differences over Gladys in a fistfight. Maybe we'd both lose a few teeth, but probably come back as pals. That's what a couple of Freemen would do. I didn't figure he was planning to get me mauled and left for dead. Mind you, that wolf of his would have done me in if I hadn't gotten to my knife in my boot. I got him good. Right across that scar of his. Thought it was a killing blow, but that wolf got back up."

"But you didn't believe me when I said my Arcwolf got back up," Ellie protested.

"Listen, recovering from a knife stab is one thing," said Ilya. "But not a rifle shot through the heart. I couldn't believe you missed it. You never miss."

"So you admit it now? I was right about the Arcwolf?" Ellie was triumphant.

"Look, I'm tired of talking," said Ilya. "I've got to go kick some Arcwolf butt. That's what I'm dealing with, right? Gabriel has been out there training himself an Arcwolf army? That's what I would have done if I was him."

"It's not an army," Sophie pushed her way past Abe to face Ilya. "Just a large pack. They just want a clear passage past the line into their sewer hunting grounds. None of the other sector commanders believed me."

"I don't believe you either," Ilya looked down at her. "Are you forgetting what happened the last time Arcwolves got past the line? Our commanders got shipped off to work the asteroids. We stopped getting recruits. It's not happening again on my watch."

"But I've got the data…" Sophie gestured behind her.

"You can have all the data you want," Ilya pushed past her. "I've got an Arcwolf army to stop."

"I already told the other commanders," Sophie kept herself in front of him. "None of them believed me that the Arcwolves were organized. I doubt you'll get any reinforcements."

"Best to try," Ilya looked back at Gladys and Ellie. "I've got to tell the linesmen..and ladies… to dig in. Ellie, I want you up in one of the towers. We'll put that kid Jeff up in the other one, but he's a wild shot compared to you. Use my old rifle with the night sight. The one that my dedushka, my grandfather had that's…"

"..mounted over your bed? I know, Papa." Ellie grabbed Abe. "You're coming with me, where I can keep you safe." She shivered. "But only after you get out of that cold suit."

20 WAR

Ilya

Sophie was right, Ilya soon discovered. None of the other commanders wanted to send their already tired linesmen for extra duty on his stretch of the wall. Even if they believed the outside chance that the Arcwolves were planning something. Even his old school pals were sympathetic but unhelpful.

"Look," said one, "if we pull our men off the line here, then we'll become the weakest sector and get overrun, da? Better call for air support from Central."

So Ilya called Central. It took forever for someone to pick up, and on the ninth try, Ilya was going to hang up when a mechanical sounding operator picked up. It asked for his business in a bored way that made Ilya want to reach through his phone and strangle the computer. Then Ilya heard the background conversation. The stupid mechanical operator didn't have the courtesy to mute him.

"Commander Plaster, Commander Patton is requesting air support for an Arcwolf attack."

"A what? Tell him the Arcwolves don't attack as a group. maybe there'll be an occasional pack, but nothing he can't handle."

The mechanical voice told Ilya this, and Ilya began swearing at it.

"He's pretty insistent, sir."

"Is he? Bring up his file. Give me a second. Oh, that's what it is. He's just been treated for radiation sickness. Guess they didn't do a good job. You know those field hospitals. Basically, dropouts given the bare minimum. Tell him he's still seeing things. Better to take some time off and see a real doctor here in World City Bela. Wait, is he still on the line? What happened to your mute function? Hello, commander?"

"You can go to hell," Ilya closed the line with a savage flick. He wanted to crush something.

Ilya had every linesman in the sha sector on alert. The wives were coming down too, arming themselves and cleaning weapons that had been sitting in closets and on mantelpieces. Ilya was staring at the faulty machine gun towers. If he dropped everyone back out of range, those two towers with their hair-trigger responses could finally be useful. They were only to be used as a last resort, but they needed all the help they could get.

"Everyone get undercover. We're not going to try and hold the wall. We'll let the automatic towers do that for us and clean up any strays." Ilya smiled. For the first time since he knew Gabriel was gunning for him, he felt like he had an advantage. "See what you think of massive automatic fire on a hair-trigger," he said to that ghostly image of Gabriel that floated out there above the Wilds. Ilya sat in the automatic tower control booth and flipped on their power grid. The towers ground to life, squealing along tracks corroded by years of acid rain, targeting anything that moved. Ilya looked out the thick window and waited.

There was no warning when the Arcwolves came. One moment there was nothing, and the next moment six Arcwolves were over the barrier, leaping over the locked gate, and streaking toward the buildings. For a moment Ilya sat spellbound at their speed and beauty.

Then the automatic towers opened up on the wolves, and they went down in a metal rain. A short howl sounded out in the Wilds. Other Arcwolves bounded back out of sight.

Silence reigned. They turned tail and disappeared, just like that? Ilya waited, but nothing happened. "That's it?" Ilya laughed. "That was your grand scheme, Gabriel? After all this time you just sent your six trained doggies up against my automatic towers? What an idiot." He swung his feet up onto the control panel and thought about what a good celebration would be for the linesmen. Maybe he could send for..movement along the line caught Ilya's eye. Lots of movement, lots of scurrying.

A wave of Skullrons poured over the wall, with Arcwolves snapping at their heels. Once over, the Skullrons poured out under the gate, through the barbed wire, over parts of the broken wall. The open space between the wall and the linesmen's quarters was soon full of a sea of tiny intruders. Most saw the open space between the two towers and made a scurrying beeline for it.

The automatic system opened up, pouring down death on the advancing wave. But the Skullrons were faster, much harder to hit. They scampered over their dead brethren and forced the automatic towers to swivel inexorably back until they were firing near the positions of the huddled linesmen.

Suddenly their salvation was tearing holes in protective walls, ricocheting into open windows, and causing panic and confusion.

"Shut them down! Shut them down." Ilya yelled. He hammered at switches, but his voice command stilled the towers. Ilya switched on the loudspeaker system. "Armor up. This just got personal." He went down to where the linesmen held behind whatever barriers they could erect.

The Arcwolves stayed well behind the Skullrons until the automatic towers ground to a halt. Then they sprang forward and met the sharpshooting of the linesmen. Too late did Ilya realize the full truth of Ellie's story about the Arcwolves. He watched with growing horror as the Arcwolves fell and rose again. Even one of the original six, riddled by the automatic guns, staggered back to its feet.

"Fall back!" Ilya called. He raced back up the stairs to the command booth. If the towers could slow the advance, his linesmen might have a chance..

Too late. The Arcwolves were in and among the linesmen, shredding their way through the line. The defensive line collapsed as the men and women fell under the weight of the wolves. The staccato of gunfire soon silenced as a stream of Arcwolves poured over the wall and out past the fallen line.

Only one rifle could be heard over the screams. Ilya heard it and knew its echo. It was his old rifle, the one his father and grandfather had used. Ellie was still firing from atop the tower, taking down Arcwolf after Arcwolf, repeating her shots as they staggered to rise.

Then the Arcwolves were through and past the line, baying and howling their way down the road into the empty alienation buffer zone of World City Bela. Ilya had failed to hold the line. His men had fallen. The Arcwolves once again roamed beyond the wall.

Ilya let the horror of his failure wash over him. When they spoke of him in the future, Frees would spit out his name. They would place it with the rest of the failed commanders, incompetents to be scorned. If they ever replaced the old urinals, his name would join the other failures in the bottom of the trough, literally pissed on for the rest of border wall history.

As Ilya felt the humiliation sink into him like a rain of molten bullets, he saw a careful figure pushing open the final locked gate and picking his way along the border wall. He'd aged, and there was a ridiculous flower growing from his gutshot wound, but there was no mistaking Gabriel.

"C-come face me!" Gabriel was using some kind of amplifying device. "Face m-me, Ilya, y-you c-coward."

Ilya had reached the control booth and flipped the automatic gun turrets back on. They swiveled to face Gabriel. Ilya smiled in his misery. At least he'd get to see his old rival chewed to pieces.

Gabriel laughed. "C-coward. Hiding behind y-your obsolete tech. Who do you think p-programmed those t-towers?" He held up a device. Ilya's console went black and one of the gun turrets swiveled to face Ilya's control booth. Ilya dived under the control panel as the gun turret tore his roof off. The barrage continued until Ilya was huddled under a shredded piece of smoking steel. Then Gabriel turned the turrets on each other. They tore into each other until they were twin pieces of smoking rubble. The silence as they finally stopped rang with the echoes of their destruction.

"F-face me, c-coward." Gabriel called.

Swearing, Ilya crawled out from under the control panel. Aside from a few burns, he was untouched by the destruction. He pushed his way through the rubble and kicked his way down the now precariously tilting outside stair.

Time to finish the job, Ilya thought. *I've lost everything, but I can still send Gabriel to hell before me.*

Ilya strode out to meet Gabriel on the Skullron strewn open area, still lit by the flood lamps of the fallen linesmen.

"Did you bring your pretty belly flower to kill me?" Ilya called. "Should've brought a gun like mine." Easily, Ilya unholstered and leveled his personal revolver at Gabriel. "Idiot 'Cyclers never have a gun when you need one."

In response, Gabriel whistled. Five dark shapes slid out of the shadows around Ilya.

"Should've b-brought more g-guns."

Ilya tried to keep the Arcwolves in front of him, but they already flanked him. "Figure you'll finish me off?" Ilya lifted his leg and unsheathed his ankle knife, holding it easily with his other hand. "I can take your doggies, Gabriel. Right after I end you." Ilya swiveled his arm up and squeezed a shot at Gabriel's head. But one of the young Arcwolves had already jumped and fastened on his arm. The shot went wide. Ilya yelled as the Arcwolf's jaws tore through his body armor. A familiar shot rang out and the Arcwolf spurted blood. It dropped off Ilya with what seemed like a mortal wound. It was Ellie, who'd climbed back up to the tower after the turrets destroyed each other and was now crouching in the tower debris.

"Ellie!" Ilya yelled. "Don't worry about me. Finish this manic."

But Gabriel was calling as well, his amplified voice drowning out Ilya's. "Ellie! You need me. You need to l-live in the Wilds. You'll d-die unless you c-come back."

Ellie's rifle stayed silent. The Arcwolves circled. Ilya cursed and wondered how he could still win.

"Stop it! Just stop it!" Both Ilya and Gabriel turned. It was Gladys, running and stumbling over the Skullron corpses. As she neared the wolf circle, the Arcwolves growled but Gabriel whistled them into silence.

"You've won, Gabriel," Gladys was weeping. "You've destroyed him. His men are dead or wounded. His name's a disgrace. You've beaten us. Don't you know you've won? Leave him alone, let him live with his humiliation."

"W-why are you d-defending him?" Gabriel turned to her. "He t-tricked you, left me for d-dead, and f-forced you to m-marry him."

"Oh, Gabriel, he didn't trick me." Gladys' tear-stained face was lined, which just made her more beautiful with a lifetime of memories. "I tried to tell you that before the two of you lunatics went off together to try and kill each other. I loved you both. I still love you both. My heart is not limited to one person. I still see the best in both of you, crazy lunatics that you are."

"Y-you can't l-love him! He's a m-murderer!"

Gladys nodded. "He tried. You both did. And yet here you both are. Now stop this. Please stop this and let me go save those that can be saved."

Gabriel stood. He seemed to shrink in on himself. "I-if that's w-what y-you r-really want, G-gladys." He whistled, and the Arcwolves reluctantly withdrew. They slunk back over the wall as if ashamed of their master.

"Good job, Gladys," Ilya smirked. "Now I can finish this traitor."

He raised his pistol.

Gabriel just looked at him. His one good eye was a pit of despair. All of Ilya's nightmares were reflected in that dark eye. Ilya willed himself to pull the trigger. But he could feel Gladys behind him. He knew pulling that trigger would be the last time she ever spoke to him. It would be the last time he'd ever sleep through the night. That soulless single eye would wake him screaming, covered in sweat, joining the dark horror of his father and grandfather in the endless muddy border nightmare that haunted him when Gladys wasn't holding him. Ilya cursed, and slowly his gun came down.

"Call your dogs out of the city," Ilya's voice was flat.

Gabriel turned and shrugged. "They're not my d-dogs. They r-ran ahead and I couldn't k-keep up. Otherwise, I w-would have t-taken out your towers before you c-could use them. But they w-wouldn't wait. Only these five y-young ones listened to me at all. And y-you saw, they don't like g-going back without a k-kill."

"We'll hunt you down, all of you," Ilya felt his control slipping.

Gabriel smiled a sad little smile. "M-maybe. N-not today." He made his slow way back through the broken gates and out beyond the wall.

Ilya turned. One of the women from the line came staggering up. She saluted. "Two dead, sir. The rest of us have been wounded. Some of the men have been bitten pretty bad."

"If you're all just wounded, why didn't you keep shooting?" Ilya rounded on the woman.

"Couldn't sir. The Arcwolves took our rifles."

21 AFTERMATH

Abe

Abe wasn't sure if it was possible to be terrified and turned on at the same time. Ellie was terrifying, but it made her beautiful and graceful at the same time. His job was to feed her bullets as fast as she slapped out her hand for more. Even with earplugs from his tool belt, his ears rang constantly.

They'd both watched the confrontation between Uncle Gabriel and Ilya. When Ilya called Ellie to end Gabriel she'd started to turn her rifle. Then she looked at Abe and returned her focus to the circling Arcwolves.

They had watched the confrontation play out in silence. When Gabriel turned to leave, Abe made a movement to follow him. Ellie caught Abe's arm and he sighed and nodded.

Now that things were quiet, Ellie looked at Abe. She put out her hand and rubbed his cheek, coming away with a dark streak of gun grease. Abe leaned into her touch, remembering her holding his injured hand all night long.

Ellie was talking, and Abe had to arch his eyebrows and pull out an earplug. "What?"

"I said, are we a thing now, deafo."

"I'm only partially deaf. And yeah, I guess we're a thing."

Ellie sat back on her haunches in the ruins of the tower. "What does that mean exactly?"

Abe shrugged. "We're dating."

Ellie grimaced and shook her head. "Frees don't date. Mama already thought I was with child. She'll be on you about getting me a gun."

"A gun?"

"Yeah, you know, an exchange of firearms to seal the deal?"

Abe looked at her sideways. "Whoa, you mean getting married?"

"Duh. Idiot."

"Abe was silent for a minute. "Isn't there something in the middle? You know, before getting married?"

Ellie snorted. "We've been out alone together too long for courting. Don't you want to get married?"

"Sure, but not right off. We've got to get the Arcwolves out of the city first."

"I bet you give all the girls the same excuse."

Abe sighed. "Fine, I'll marry you."

Ellie shook her head. "No, I don't want to marry you anymore. You missed your chance."

"Hey, that's not fair. You can't back out."

"Sure I can. I'm the girl. I change my mind all the time. Look it up."

"OK," Abe stood up. "We're just a thing for right now. I need to go find my mom. I think she knows where the Arcwolves went."

Ellie poked him. "Don't you know? I thought you knew everything."

"Well, I have an idea."

"What's your idea?"

"I think they're in the sewers."

"Why would they be in the sewers?"

"I think they've gone to find their relatives. My mom said something about how there used to be an open channel and your grandpa cut it off."

"Figures we'd get blamed. So they're not going to go eat all the employees?"

"No." Abe shook his head in annoyance. "Wolves, even Arcwolves, don't eat people. They eat Skullrons." He patted a bump under his null suit. "Not you, Cyrano. They eat Skullrons and plants. There are lots of both in the Wilds. I guess down in the sewers they'd eat Rateons and whatever grows down there."

Ellie screwed up her face. "What's a Rateon?"

"Oh, that's right. You've never been into the World City because you're not an employee."

"Neither have you. You've been stuck here on the border, same as me."

"That's not true. My parents brought me into World City Bela once. My dad had to get his World City paperwork because he wasn't officially recognized until he was an adult. I saw Rateons, which are a little like long-tailed Skullrons with feathers. They can kind of fly and hop. My mom was going to let me touch one, but my dad said it wasn't relevant to the task at hand."

"You really hate him, don't you?"

"My dad? No, I just hate his attitude. Nothing fun is ever relevant."

Ellie stood up and pulled Abe up with her. She kissed him. He tried to say something through their lips, then kissed her back.

Ellie pulled away and wiggled her eyebrows at Abe. "Am I relevant?"

"Yes! I mean...I don't know. It doesn't matter. I'm not my dad."

"It very much does matter." Ellie stepped close to him.

Abe looked at her. His mind was blank. "I'm supposed to think of something clever, but I can't think. You smell sweaty and good."

"That's the right answer," said Ellie. She kissed him again.

Ellie

Ellie descended the stairs before Abe. It hadn't looked like any of the Arcwolves had gone into any of the buildings. But Ellie wasn't taking chances with her new boyfriend.

Was that what he was? She couldn't decide. Abe didn't fit the spot that Todd had filled in her for so long. Trying to stuff Abe into her dream of being a perfect Free wife didn't work. He was an unknown, a warm patch in her chest, a hunger in her belly. Or maybe that was just hunger.

"I'm starving," Ellie called up to Abe. "It's weird because I ate not too long ago."

"You need radiation," Abe called down to her. "Pick up some dead Skullrons. Some of them should be pretty hot."

When Ellie pushed on the door outside she had to shove little Skullron bodies out of the way. One of them looked better than the others, warmer.

Abe saw her eyeing the Skullron. "Touch it."

Ellie reached out and cradled the little body. "It's warm."

"No," Abe stepped around her. "It's radioactive. Here." He pulled a flattened "Cycler rag sack out of his coveralls. "Fill up this sack with warm Skullrons."

"You carry sacks around with you all the time?" Ellie looked at him.

Abe grinned. "I'm a 'Cycler. We're always ready to recycle things we find. It's like Frees always carrying around guns. Part of our society. Besides, they double as insulation." He pulled another sack out of the other pants leg. "I'll help you so people don't realize what you're doing. I don't think even your family realizes you need radiation to live now. I don't know have you've survived this long."

Ellie thought and blushed. "I ate Papa's radiation."

Abe nodded. "Probably saved both of you, then."

Once Ellie started paying attention, she could pick out the hottest Skullrons. Most were cool. A few were warm, and very few were really hot. She filled up her bag with warm and hot ones, resisting the urge to hug the bag.

Abe saw her indecision and swung his bag over his back. Ellie followed suit. She basked in the radiation, soaking it in like a heating pad.

Sophie came up to the two of them. "Be careful! If the Skullrons have just eaten they're likely to be very radioactive."

"Nah," Abe waved her off. "I checked. All cool. You can check my bag if you want."

"Sophie pulled her Geiger counter from her tool belt. "I did not just get you back to lose you to the radiation ward with blisters, buster. Turn around." She ran her Geiger up and down his sack. "Hmmm...they are cool. Ellie, you next."

"No!" Abe tried to get in the way.

Sophie looked at him. "Abraham Michael Franklin King, you haven't been able to fool me since you were six. What are the two of you up to? And don't tell me you just want to clean up. There are still linesmen hurt over there. Though the Arcwolves were as gentle as they could be. Frees just don't like to give up their guns. What's going on?"

Ellie pulled her sack of Skullrons in front of her and hugged it, pulling at the radiation. "Please, Ms. King, I need them." She drew the warmth into her as fast as she could.

Sophie stepped around Abe and scanned Ellie. "Why in Einstein's name would you need a bag of hot Skullrons?" She shook her Geiger counter and scanned again. "Why...I think my Geiger counter is broken. The reading keeps dropping."

"Wow," Abe was looking over his mom's shoulder. "You're just absorbing it. It's practically just stray particles. Ellie, can you turn around?"

Ellie turned slowly, still holding her Skullrons and drawing the warmth into herself.

"Look," Abe was excited. "Nothing but background. She's as good as the new null suit we left back in our apartment."

"Well," Sophie looked at both of them, "as much as I'd like the story of how Ellie became a radioactive Skullron-needing null suit, we need to figure out where all the Arcwolves went. Central will be demanding an update. The other sector commanders must have heard the automatic towers firing. I held them off with a quick security tape recording of those six Arcwolves downed by the automatic towers. But once Commander Patton regains his sanity he'll call in a catastrophic breach report. That means sha sector command switches to Central. Every gunship border security can get up the air will be coming our way. Not to mention hovers full of gun-crazed Dubsee Free faddists who track our communication and would love to use their weapons in a real firefight. We'll likely even get a visit from the Three in charge of energy production. If that zoo doesn't scatter the combined packs all over World City Bela, I don't know what will.

"Abe, I need you to drive a hover. Do you still remember how?"

Abe bit his lip. "It's been a while..."

Sophie cut him off. "Of course you do. You loved the simulator. Practiced crashing into everything. I don't need perfection, I just need someone who knows how not to run into things. Ellie, since you're part of the Abe package now, come along. I'd say bring your rifle, but that's assumed. Can you use an infrared scanner?"

"Uh…" Ellie wasn't sure which scanner that was. It had only been a day's training in the border school. "Cyclers handled the scanners."

"Of course, you can." Sophie pursed her lips. "It's just a rifle without bullets. Let's go."

22 SEARCH

Abe

The sha sector hover, so unused it was usually covered with the gray dust of the world city, was also partially covered with bits of the exploded gun tower that had rained down on the hoverpad.

"We're lucky it wasn't blown up," Sophie said as she pushed past the debris and opened the hover hatch. "I suppose we'd have 'cycled it just the same."

Abe buckled himself in and started up the hover. Ellie sat next to him, still holding her bag of Skullrons. Abe had discarded his bag somewhere on the way up.

Sophie rummaged around in an equipment bag until she came up with an ancient infrared scanner. "We bought this back when we were first moving to the line." Sophie held out the scanner to Ellie. "That's before Abe was born. We thought it would be useful to track things at the border It took a day for us to realize that the radiation of the Wilds would make it so confusing it'd be worthless. The only infrared that works is the very short range like on your rifle scopes. Look," she held up the scanner for Ellie, "just point and scan. Look for a pile of Arcwolves streaming along a sewer line. I know the broken grate where they went in. I just need the sewer schematics and the scanner to figure out where they've gone."

"How do you know where they went in?" Abe asked as he brought the hover up to a shaky start and then a simulation perfect climb.

Sophie was bringing up the schematics on the 3D workbench and reached over to hug him. "God it's good to have you back. How do you think I know, my bright boy?"

Abe reasoned. "You broke open a storm drain, destroyed a grate, and made sure the Arcwolves found it?"

Sophie smiled. "Let's just say that I lost an acetylene torch I checked out of supply and have no idea what happened to five kilos of fake meat, that fungi-grown stuff. It might have ended up as a sort of Arcwolf runway down into that open sewer drain. Head straight toward the first two-miler. Most of the old sewer lines run in that direction. Ellie, you're going to need to scan with two hands."

"No ma'am." Ellie shook her head. "I trained both my wrists for full rifle weight even before...I got stronger." Ellie glanced at Abe.

"Don't bother," said Abe as he steered the hover toward the far-off two-miler over the alienation zone. "Mom will figure it out if she hasn't already. Mom, Ellie's got the new mitochondria that run on radiation."

"Like the Skullrons?" Sophie was absorbed in her schematics. "I suppose that's how Gabriel survived. Go left here, honey. Track along the left side of the old road. Anything yet, Ellie?"

"No ma'am."

Sophie glanced up at Ellie. "I like her, Abe. She's way more polite than most 'Cycler girls."

Abe looked up with alarm. "Mom! It's not like I've brought home any 'Cycler girls."

"I know, honey. Honestly, I was getting a little worried. Not about your preference, just about your confidence. I've known your preference since you were ten."

Abe sighed. "I don't want to know how."

"Well, you don't encrypt your searches, honey." Sophie looked over at Ellie for support. "It's a little surprising to be searching the work table interface for cute booties to go with an outfit and get served a dozen ads for large bottomed women."

Ellie laughed.

"Don't worry, dear," Sophie smiled at her. "His tastes are quite...eclectic. You fall well within his taste spectrum."

"Good to know," Ellie laughed again at Abe's humiliation.

"I could crash this hover right now," Abe looked over at his mom.

"But you won't, dear. It isn't in your perfectionist nature. I'm almost done." Sophie turned to Ellie and then back at her schematics. "The reason I was worried about Abe is that he has such perfectionistic tendencies. I thought he might never find anyone who met his standards. It speaks very highly of you. See dear, I'm complimenting your girlfriend."

"Not to change the subject, mom, but let's change the subject."

Sophie smiled at Ellie. "Very well, dear, let's try this right turn up ahead. Three of the main sewage lines have a reservoir up ahead. Anything, Ellie?"

Ellie scanned, taking slow sweeps like she would with her rifle. "Nothing. No...wait...there's one heat signature."

Abe slowed the hover.

Sophie watched the signature. "It could be a Wanderer. I don't know what one would be doing this far out into the alienation zone. No, that's a three-legged gait. It looks pretty badly wounded. Did any of those first six Arcwolves get up again?"

Ellie nodded. "Only five stayed down."

"I bet that's her." Sophie smiled. "So we're on the right track. Scan ahead."

Ellie ran the infrared ahead as they outpaced the first Arcwolf. They passed several other stragglers and soon they had a steady stream of bodies, all hidden well below street level.

An alarm went off on one of Sophie's screens. "Drat," she said. "Patton's deputy Jacob is trying to file a catastrophic breach with Central. Lucky for us, he doesn't have Ilya's override access. I patched into sha sector communications and rerouted all outgoing calls through this hover. He has to go through me. Everyone quiet for a moment."

Sophie assumed her blandest tone. "Thank you for contacting Central. How may I assist you?"

"The Arcwolves are in the city! There's been a catastrophic breach! I'm…"

"Sir," Sophie cut him off, "we are aware of the situation. The Arcwolves have already been corralled. They are in the process of being contained. Thank you for calling."

"Oh, Thank Einstein! I've been so worried…"

"Sir, can I recommend checking in for a psych evaluation? You sound quite distraught. We need every lineman ready for work tomorrow."

"You're right. It's been very stressful. Commander Ilya hasn't been available. I usually have to handle all the paperwork, but just the reports. I've never had to command anyone before. The linemen don't listen to me unless I yell at them. One of them even laughed at me. Laughed at his commanding officer! Well, I did squeak when I yelled. But that's no excuse. I had to discipline…"

"Thank you for calling," Sophie broke into his ramble. "I have another call coming in."

"Oh, of course. I'm sorry. Goodbye."

Sophie got off the call and smiled and Ellie and Abe. "That should buy us some time. Anything new, Ellie?"

Ellie nodded. "There's a whole lot of signatures coming up." Ellie repositioned the scanner. "That's a lot of Arcwolves. Abe, can you take us lower? I'm losing the bottom of the signal."

Abe dropped them down lower to the silent empty blocks of the alienation zone and glanced at Ellie's scanner. "Are we sure they aren't people? Maybe a gathering of Wanderers? If that scanner is right, that's got to be hundreds of signatures."

"We're still in the alienation zone here," said Sophie. "This whole area had an enforced evacuation because of concerns of radiation leakage dating back to before the two milers went up. If anyone in Central had any sense, the border wall would be out beyond this zone. But that would admit we're constantly losing ground to the Wilds. So why would the Wanderers decide to risk radiation when they could have gathered safely in World City Bela? Besides, there aren't that many Wanderers. They usually get taken by the Cullers soon after their unemployment hearings for some minor crime and sent out to the asteroid belt. No," she watched the scan. "Those are Arcwolves. Probably a mix of the group from the Wilds with the wolves who've been living in the pipes all these years."

"Look," Ellie focused on the scanner. "There's an open area with two signatures in the middle. Abe, hold us steady."

Abe punched the controls and the hover hung in the grey pre-dawn sky.

Ellie watched the two circling signatures. "It's a combat, isn't it?"

Sophie nodded. "Likely two Alpha males deciding who will lead. If Scar is one of them, I pity the other."

The three watched as the two signatures moved. Ellie focused the scanner down so that only the two signatures appeared large in the scope viewing screen.

"Well, maybe not pity," said Sophie. "If the scanner's readings are correct, that thing's a monster. At least as big as a bear. We'll see how this goes."

The larger signature lunged for the smaller. While the smaller shape seemed not to respond, the larger shape fell back and went still."

Sophie whistled. "You can't let a Wilds Arcwolf like Scar build up that much charge. It shocked them both, but the big one isn't used to it. Let's see if he gets back up."

The two signatures were still for a few moments, then the larger one moved. But instead of approaching the other signature, it backed away until only one of the signatures stood in the empty circle.

"One pack, one leader," said Sophie. "I wonder what his plan is for the recovered pack?"

"Identify yourself!" The harsh sound cut through their hover speaker system with the high-pitched squeal of a security override.

All three of them looked up. While they had been occupied, a hover had quietly descended and now hovered next to them.

Sophie swore under her breath. She breathed deep and made her voice flat, slow and clear. "Sophia Tanya King, sha sector security observation, and my...children."

"Current mission?" The voice could have been automatic, Abe thought, one of the old audio interfaces that didn't try to fool you with a human-sounding voice.

Sophie sucked in her breath. "We had some trouble with the Arcwolves last night. I'm just being thorough and scanning to make sure we got them all."

There was a pause. "We have no record of an incident from last night. There were reports from other sectors, but nothing from the sha sector. Central did request an update."

"Oh? Well, yes," Sophie sounded surprised. "I'm sure it's just a communications delay."

"Probably," the voice sounded bored. "Are you done with your scan or do you need assistance? This hover has the latest scanners."

"No!" Sophie's voice sounded too alarmed and went up too high. "We're done. Heading back now. No need to make more paper work for both of us."

There was another pause. "Stay where you are, please." The voice had lost its bored tone. "I'm scanning the area."

"Listen, officer, there's no need…"

"Please maintain silence until the scan is complete."

The three of them waited in silence.

"Begin scanning back toward the border wall. Wait. I'm picking up a single heat signature. Please stay in place while I investigate." The security hover lifted away from them and went back the way they'd come.

23 CAUGHT

Ellie

Ellie looked at Sophie, who put her finger to her lips and motioned to the infrared scanner. Ellie scanned the area below them. It was cold! Where had all the Arcwolves gone?

Behind them, there was an explosion. To Ellie'scombat simulation trained ear, it sounded like a micro-buster, something meant to penetrate into the ground. It was followed by the sound of automatic fire. A moment later, the speaker system crackled as the security hover took control again. "You missed one. I breached the upper sewer pipe and ended it. But we'll need a clean-up crew and a full report."

"Thank you," said Sophie. "We'll head back now."

"I don't think so. Central is going to want an accounting of my use of extreme measures in the alienation zone. Explosives don't grow on trees. I'm going to need witnesses. Please follow me."

"But we need to…"

"Miz King, don't make me tractor your hover. Sorry, it's been a long night, but I've got to answer some tough questions. I can't answer them without you with me. Follow me back to Central. That is not a request."

Abe

Abe wasn't used to seeing his mom at a loss for words. Sophie stayed silent while he piloted their hover behind the security hover.

The hovers slid over the silent streets. Most of the streets were in poor repair, decaying under the acid rains with no crews to undo the damage. But as they approached the two-miler, occasionally Abe saw lights in the officially abandoned homes. He knew that Wanderers squatted in some of the abandoned buildings at the edge of the alienation zone. Periodic raids by security Cullers refilled the prison ships heading out to the asteroid belt.

Ahead of them was a stream of light, extending up and down as far as the eye could see. It was just a glow from the edge of the evacuation zone, but as they got closer it got even brighter. Thousands of hovers, traveling at preset levels, streamed past each other in a dance-like motion. Beyond them rose the first of the two milers, a great squat curving structure that arched up and up until it disappeared into the gray clouds. The upper levels were populated by the elite of the world city, living above the clouds in the sunlight with whole floors dedicated to gardens. They were the only ones able to see the stars above the gray clouds that blocked out the sky for most of the poorer residents of World City Bela.

As they reached the border of the lights, the speaker system crackled. "Please stay within a hover length as we pass out of the alienation zone. I recommend auto-track engaging if your hover has that feature. We're heading to Central unit 60739, level 1366."

Abe was glad for the warning. He'd been panicking, looking out at the endless stream of hovers. Simulations and driving over the empty alienation zone were one thing. Navigating the chaos that was World City Bela's traffic was another. He put the security hover as his auto-track target, then pulled closer and engaged auto-tracking.

Glancing over, Abe saw Ellie transfixed. She looked like she was both entranced and terrified. He had a sudden urge to protect her, to hide her away inside his coveralls like Cyrano. It was ridiculous because she was the last person who needed protection. But she looked over at him and he saw her take a deep breath. Ellie reached out her hand and Abe gripped it. They both smiled.

Sophie reached past Abe and turned on the internal music system. She scrolled through the choices until she found some disturbing atonal throat singers. Abe looked at her like she was crazy. Even he didn't like this off-world garbage. Sophie motioned to him and Ellie, pulling them close together. "We saw nothing. That's all we have to say." She reached over to Ellie's scanner and motioned to Abe. he saw that she needed a hex key to unfasten the casing. Reaching down, Abe felt a surge of satisfaction. The hex key he pulled up from his tool belt was the very same one he had to replace when he lost it during the incident with Scar, so long ago. Finally, his obsession with a perfect tool belt was paying off.

Abe undid the backing of the scanner and Sophie took the scanner apart. She pulled out the scanner central processor, removed it, and handed Abe the scanner and backing. Undoing the processor, Sophie flicked out the memory crystals onto her palm. She handed Abe the processor and pocketed the crystals. Abe replaced the processor and the backing. Ellie watched them both in silence.

The two hovers slid along between streams of traffic. Pulsating lights on the security hover cleared the way before them.

The alienation and border wall Central tower was black and squat, sitting like a toadstool next to the foot of the rising tree that was the two-miler.

As they came closer Abe got a sick feeling in his stomach. Banks of automatic turrets rusted on the roof, weapons left over from the end of the Corporate Wars. Security hovers parked below them, so many that they crowded under the turrets. The security hover they were following had to circle three sides of the tower until they found two open spaces together. So many security officers, Abe thought to himself. Surely some of them will be put on me for interrogation. He tried imagining how long he could resist. Not as long as Ellie or his mom, he was sure.

Ellie

Despite her time with Abe, Ellie had been shocked when she realized that Abe's mother Sophie was planning to cover up the Arcwolf gathering. Ellie knew that the 'Cyclers felt far more for the Arcwolves than the Frees. She just hadn't thought that love extended to hiding the Arcwolves' movements inside the world city. But Ellie had stayed silent because Sophie had asked. She wasn't sure how long she could remain silent if they started questioning her. So far it had just been a case of not telling the officer what she knew. If he asked directly, Ellie wasn't sure what she would do.

When they landed, the security officer waited for them to come out of their hover. Ellie couldn't see his face inside his mirrored helmet. But his uniform showed a very high rank. Far too high a rank to have been out on a routine patrol. He led them to the stairs at the top of the tower. Despite being dwarfed by the two-miler, this station towered above the alienation zone and gave them a view of the brown smudge of the Wilds in the distance over the darkness of the evacuated alienation zone.

A long, echoing descent led them out into a vast floor full of shadowy, empty cubicles. They were asked to sit in one of the corner offices and the officer found them three working chairs, but the security officer was unable to get any of the monitors to function. In frustration, he told them to wait while he got one of the portable reporting units.

When the officer left, Abe looked around the empty, shabby office and whispered, "What is going on here?"

Ellie knew. "It's a freeze-out." This is how sector commanders were forced to resign. "When a no-good commander needs to resign, they transfer away everyone else. All the equipment is allowed to fail. Eventually, the commander accepts a demotion and a lower position in another sector. This one seems to not be getting the message."

Sophie looked around and nodded. "I've never seen one this bad. Usually, they give up while they still have employees."

"No wonder no one ever got back to Papa," Ellie shook her head. "He said they used to respond from Central like regular people. But there's been no answer for years. I wonder how long this commander has held out?"

"Judging from the breakdown of this equipment," Sophie tilted one of the monitors, "more than a few years."

"But he can't be alone," said Abe. "He was out on patrol. Wasn't he talking to someone here at Central?"

"Automatic recording," said Ellie. "It helps border patrols file paperwork. You just call it in and the system writes it up. All you need to do at the end of the shift is sign off."

Abe was unconvinced. "What about all those hovers on the roof?"

Ellie shrugged. "Who knows how many still work? None of them looked like they were newer than our border hover. He's driving the only recent hover he's got."

Sophie looked out over the empty cubicles. "He's been gone a long time. Where did he go?"

Ellie pointed to the elevators, which stood partially open and dark. "He probably has to take the stairs. In a place like this, that could be a lot of flights down to a supply floor."

"Wow," Abe walked out into the darkened hallway and looked out at the line of silent cubicles. "How incompetent do you have to be to get this treatment?"

"Not very," said the security officer behind him.

"Gleep!" Abe spun around and swung his elbow at the security guard's head. The guard barely blocked it with the portable recording device which spun out of his hands and cracked on the floor when it landed. Ellie was momentarily very proud of Abe for not collapsing into a faint.

"Sorry," Abe managed.

"Don't be," said the officer. "My fault entirely for surprising you. Nice reflexes, by the way."

"Amazing reflexes!" Said Sophie. "Abe, baby, where did you learn to do that?"

"Oh, Ellie and I fight all the time," said Abe. "I mean, not fight, but…"

"I understand," said Sophie. "Ellie, I love what you've done to my boy. Did you know one time I surprised him from behind and he went into his faint routine at the top of a flight of stairs? As a mother, I didn't know whether to scream or laugh as he bumped his way down. Luckily he didn't break any bones, but…"

"Mom! Could we not tell embarrassing stories about me for once? We've got security reports to do."

"Not with this machine anymore," said the security officer, turning over the newly cracked portable. "But I do want to hear your report. I need to pass it on to my superior officer, commander Reginald Archimedes Plaster. Or, as you've already guessed, me." He flipped up his mirrored visor and unfastened his helmet, revealing a thin face with high cheekbones and surprisingly large, dark eyes.

"Are you the only one here?" Abe couldn't help himself.

"Yes, I'm afraid so," Reginald looked over the empty office. "Only the top floors are empty. The rest of the building is energy supply division offices. They cut off my elevator access and transferred my last employee away from me last week." He looked at their faces.

"Oh, I know you're all wondering what colossal incompetence on my part triggered a freeze-out? I only wish it was that easy." He sighed. "I'm sure you've heard the rumors, but it's not true that I embezzled patrol funds. I can't prove it, but I was tracking credit transfers to my commanding Four. Then my files went blank and I've been in freeze-out since. That was…a long time ago."

"Can't you just transfer?" asked Ellie.

"It's never been offered," said Reginald. "My only option is to resign, to voluntarily become a Wanderer. There's a Culler who checks on me every day, waiting for me to give up." He glanced at the darkened elevator shaft. "I don't think I'd last very long on the asteroid belt."

Ellie looked at the small man, his hair receding and graying at the temples. His uniform was still perfect, and he held himself straight, but she could see the tension in the lines of his face. He smelled of desperation.

"But enough about me," Reginald glanced around at them. "Tell me about this catastrophic breach you're trying to cover up."

"What?" Abe and Sophie reacted together. Ellie had to smile.

"Oh, I was up at your hover,' Reginald explained. "I was looking at your scanner, but someone had removed the memory crystals. So I listened to the automatic recording system every hover has on whenever it's running."

Sophie put her hand to her face. "The auto-record. I should have pulled the auto-record."

Reginald nodded. "It's a common oversight by amateur criminals. Most professionals carry a universal jamming device that makes the recordings just static."

"Are those easy to make?" Abe was interested.

"Surprisingly so," said Reginald. "They just broadcast at all licensed frequencies. I've often said we should manufacture security listening devices at non-published frequencies. But you can't get any new ideas up through to the top of W.C. Central. I do know that you're not professionals, you're just amateurs. It won't matter since the crime is an attempted cover-up of a catastrophic breach."

"Please," said Sophie. "I take full responsibility. The kids were just along for the ride."

"Well, said Reginald, "they'd still be accomplices. Same penalty."

Sophie looked stricken. "So we're all going to the asteroid belt?"

"Perhaps," said Reginald. "Remember, I'm not far off from the belt myself. Thanks to your large son, I can't even record our conversation. What's remarkable to me is that there's nothing on the feeds, secure or public, about a catastrophic breach. You'd think if the Arcwolves were tearing the world city populace apart it would at least show up on a gossip feed. So where did they all go?"

Abe and Sophie looked at each other.

Ellie stood up straight. "Commander Plaster, sir, I want to report a catastrophic breach in the sha sector of the border wall. An unspecified number of Arcwolves overran our defenses and made their way into the city, congregating in an underground reservoir area. Afterward, they disappeared."

"Thank you," said Reginald. "Do you want a job?" "I don't believe you're hiring, sir."

"No, but if I play this right, I might be. Nothing breaks a freeze-out like being a hero." He looked at the three of them. "Of course, I would report that the brave border patrol guards tracked the Arcwolves to an underground reservoir after immediately signaling to Central security. We…I…met you at the scene. As I am the only current zone security guard in this region, that fact alone should make heads roll. After the Arcwolves disappeared, we left an automatic infrared tracker at the point of the last contact and returned to the Central alienation zone headquarters to plan our counter-attack."

"But we didn't leave a tracker," Abe pointed out.

"You didn't leave a tracker, I did," replied Reginald. "I also have your recording from your hover to prove that the call was made. Turns out I was forced to deputize this lady here to take my calls as I was already en route to intercept." Reginald bit his lip. "I hope our excavator still works. Otherwise, we have to put on null suits and retrieve that Arcwolf carcass by hand. If it works, I have more than enough tunnel bubble for it. By Einstein, I've got enough for the entire border wall. Pretty sick joke by my commanding Four. I asked for a hundred meters worth, and he used my entire budget to send me hundreds of tubes. The entire third floor is full of tunnel bubble tubes. Enough to stretch from here to the border wall and back." He smiled. "So even though I've got no staff and only broken equipment, we're over budget for the quarter. If I complain, I'll look greedy and inefficient."

Sophie looked at Reginald. "So you're willing to lie about what's happening to save your own skin?"

Reginald shook his head. "I'm doomed. My Four will make sure I go down sooner or later. But I can make his life difficult, maybe even get him demoted. It's worth it to me because I'll have a smile on my face when they ship me off to the belt.

"You, on the other hand," Reginald pointed to them in turn. "Are genuine heroes. Provided we can do something that rids world city of an Arcwolf invasion. I figure you must have a plan."

"Not really," Sophie shrugged. "My big victory was getting them down into the sewers rather than rampaging the streets. I was hoping they'd come back the same way."

"Back through sha sector?" Ellie was aghast. "Papa will lose his mind. The barracks can't become an Arcwolf highway."

Sophie bristled. "It's his fault his own grandfather blew up their natural tunnel. And I'm afraid your father hasn't got much of a mind left to lose."

"Papa is trying to keep all of us safe. He's not the best at keeping his temper, but he…"

"Hey!" said Abe. "Not that I don't love that my mom and my…girlfriend -that sounds weird- " he looked over at Ellie. "Not that I don't mind them arguing, but why don't we rebuild the tunnel?" Sophie and Ellie looked at him, more out of surprise that he'd spoken up than his idea.

"If I understand," said Reginald, "you're saying that there used to be a tunnel that allowed the Arcwolves access into the sewers of World City Bela. So they could run free through the streets?"

"Not through the streets," said Sophie. "Deep under the streets. Before the newest two-miler water and sewage recovery methods, there were pipes everywhere, even connecting the towns in the Wilds to the main city. When the two milers were being built, there were massive deep reservoirs for rainwater. They used to let the rain just pour down the sides. It was like getting hit with a waterfall. That was before the rain was collected in all the sill collectors, cleaned, and 'cycled at the level of collection. So the huge reservoirs under the two milers are mostly empty now. I think that's where the Arcwolves roam around. The place has to be crawling with rateons, Skullrons, teethers, slithers, octi, and even shamblers. It's a polluted underground ecosystem that likely rivals the population on the surface."

"If it's as vast as you say," pointed out Reginald, "how would we ever locate the Arcwolves?"

"We don't need to," said Sophie. "They'll stay safe under the city, deeper than standard infrared can detect. The only problem is whether they want to return to the Wilds. Currently, the only way back is through the sha sector. So we'll have a reverse catastrophic breach at some point."

"That doesn't sound good." Reginald brushed an imaginary piece of lint off his uniform.

"It will probably happen under new leadership. Once word of this gets out Commander Patton is likely to be shipped off-world. Sorry, Ellie." Sophie turned.

Reginald thought. "A new Commander being attacked by Arcwolves from inside the city? They'd lose their minds. It would lead to a massive, unbalanced response."

Sophie nodded. "They'd have to bomb the Wilds."

"Would that work?" Abe wondered.

"It didn't the last two times they tried it. Mostly it destabilizes the radioactive waste and causes it to migrate to a wider area. We lost entire towns because the Wilds spread so rapidly. But I'm sure they'll do it again."

"Why?" asked Abe. "It didn't work. That would be illogical."

"It still makes sense if you're scared," said Ellie. "Anything is better than being scared and doing nothing." Reginald looked at Sophie. "So if we could build a tunnel into the Wilds and seal off the sewers in the Alienation Zone, then the Arcwolves will effectively disappear? They'd never bother world city? No running amok in the streets? Just deep down in those old reservoirs and then back into the Wilds?"

"It should work," Sophie frowned. "Before Ilya's grandfather blew up the tunnels, there were no reports of Arcwolves at the wall for years. That's why they went out with hunting parties, to prove the Arcwolves still existed. They needed to justify the existence of the border Frees. There was a lot of discussion about disbanding the Frees, so the Frees would take high-level employees on Arcwolf hunts. They'd have a caged Arcwolf starving near the hunt site. When the employees came the Frees would give them special repellant clothing which had really been soaked in Skullron blood. Drove the Arcwolves crazy. They'd come snapping at the hunting blinds. The employees would be shocked and terrified, begging for the Frees to protect them. The higher-ups would agree to continue Free funding without question. Just keep those crazy Arcwolves away from us. It was all an act for their benefit."

"Listen," said Reginald, "I get that you think the fuzzy little Arcwolves are harmless. But my superiors think they are terrors out to destroy World City Bela. So I can't tell them the Arcwolves probably won't attack. I have to tell them the Arcwolves have been destroyed."

"If we collapse the upper tunnels where we last saw them," said Abe, "wouldn't that stop them?"

"Maybe," said Sophie. "But they will find another way. It's best to make it easier to go back out into the Wilds. If we pave the way for them out into sunlight and Skullrons, why would they want to come up anywhere in the world city where there's concrete and no food?"

"Don't forget the lower production levels of the two milers," said Reginald. "Lots of livestock there."

"No," said Sophie. "Despite all the myths, that's not the preferred Arcwolf diet. For far less effort and risk an Arcwolf could have a dozen Skullrons and a full belly. They only hunt larger prey on rare occasions."

"All right," said Reginald. "I agree to build a tunnel if we also plant explosives in the upper tunnels, at least near where you last saw the

Arcwolves heading deeper. We'll use the explosion to back up my announcement that the Arcwolves have been destroyed. I just hope you're right about their behavior."

"If I'm not," said Sophie, "sha sector will be in a lot more trouble than you are."

"Great," said Reginald. "We can all keep each other company mining in the outer belt. Let's get my excavator going and start this tunnel. Does anyone else need an expresso bar to stay awake?" He pulled several food bars from a desk drawer. "I don't get much sleep these days."

24 TUNNELING

Abe

They spent the next few hours transferring tunnel-bubble into their two hovers. Reginald claimed many of the other hovers worked, he just didn't trust most of their automatic guidance systems on autopilot.

"I don't know if you've ever seen a tunnel-bubble explosion," he told Abe as they maneuvered a full pallet of tunnel-bubble on a mini-hover dolly up the stairs to the roof. "It's like a firework that gets frozen and then comes crashing down like a cement block on anything below it."

"How do you know?" asked Abe.

"Oh," Reginald looked away. "Someone I know might have used tunnel-bubble for target practice when he was a new recruit in the Alienation Zone. He could have been a great marksman assigned to excavation duty and a bit out of his mind with boredom. The tunnel bubble might have landed on his excavator and gotten him assigned to desk duty even though they couldn't prove it hadn't been a freak accident."

Abe looked at the tunnel-bubble canisters. "So what kind of bullet penetrates those canisters?"

"Rifle, handgun. Anything bigger than a .22. Those ricochet right off," Reginald caught himself. "So I've been told."

"Good to know," said Abe.

Once they'd put in enough tunnel-bubble to fill the excavator many times over, the slow parade of hovers moved back off the roof. They slid between the endless lines of traffic, lights flashing. Piloting the border hover, Abe was amazed that so many people could be around him, and still he felt so alone.

Well, not alone. Ellie had come with him while Sophie had ridden in the first hover with Reginald. Two more hovers bobbed behind them on auto-tractor like they were balloons on a string.

Abe remembered balloons, these odd pieces of blown-up plastic that his mom had gotten him when she wasn't as pure a 'Cycler as she was now.

"Do you want to fool around or something?" Ellie asked him.

"No, what?" Abe blushed, darkening his already dark complexion.

"It's just that you've been staring at my legs for like three minutes," said Ellie. "I figured maybe it was a 'Cycler hint that you wanted to fool around."

"No," said Abe. "I was thinking about balloons."

"Oh, right," said Ellie, "my balloons. I get it. Frees are taught to block out those thoughts because they distract. But I guess 'Cyclers just let them hang out."

"Hang out? You think I'm thinking about that all the time?" Abe checked their course and made sure his tracker was locked on the security hover. Then he turned to face Ellie.

"Pretty much," said Ellie. "Todd said he thought about it and had to suppress it every day. Especially when he was around me and we were alone. I figured it was the same for you."

"We've been alone a bunch of times," said Abe.

"I know," said Ellie. "Ages in the lab. It was pretty intense. Even I had to suppress it when you were around, especially when we were sparring."

"When we were sparring?"

"Yeah, when we were grabbing each other, all sweaty. That's when it really bothers me and I have to suppress it."

Abe shook his head. "I don't suppress it."

"I know," said Ellie. "That's why you were staring at my legs and talking about balloons."

"Kids," said Sophie's voice cut through the hover-to-hover intercom. "I don't think we need to hear your intimate discussions. Can you put yourselves on mute? Thanks!"

"Mom!" Abe slapped the mute button. He looked at Ellie. "Do you really think 'Cycler boys just think about - you know - all the time?"

"Don't you?" Ellie looked at him and leaned forward. "Todd said Free boys all do. They have to take cold showers at least once a day. 'Cyclers are always dating, so I figure it must be worse for you."

Abe thought. "I guess maybe we do think about it a lot, but that doesn't mean we're...look, 'Cyclers can date, but I've never dated anyone."

"You haven't? I figured you'd been with most of the 'Cycler girls."

"No! Look, just because you can do something doesn't mean you do. The two other 'Cycler guys I know just talk about dating. None of us have done anything."

"Wow." Ellie looked at him. "That's not what Free cadets think. We all figured you were like animals. Basically everyone with everyone."

"Ew! Gross!" Abe couldn't help himself.

"I know," said Ellie. "You can imagine how gross it was when I started to think about you at all like that. It was like wanting to use a sleeping roll that everyone else has already slept in."

"Yuck. Thanks for that image," said Abe. He was silent. "So why do you even like me at all?"

Ellie rubbed her face. "You make me feel safe. Not safe like Papa, safer in a better way. You were nice to me even when you knew I'd tried to kill you. Plus you saved my life. Lots of reasons. Come to think of it, why do you like me? Are you into would-be murderers?"

"I've always liked you." It was out before Abe could stop it. He took a deep breath. "You've always been what I'm not. Confident, fearless, gorgeous. You're totally in your body, like a pure animal. I'm just stuck in my head."

"So you showed me your little mutant chipmunk pet because you liked me?" Ellie asked.

As if he knew he was being discussed, Cyrano poked his head out of the top of Abe's coveralls. "Yeah," said Abe.

"Hi Cyrano," said Ellie. "Sorry for snitching on you and almost getting you killed."

"Did you just apologize, again?" Abe turned toward the controls. "I wish I hadn't muted out my mom. Nobody is going to believe me."

"Shut up," said Ellie. She carefully grabbed the front of his coveralls and kissed him. Cyrano chittered and ran for the control panel. But Abe wasn't as surprised and kissed her back.

"Heads up, kids," said Sophie over the intercom, "we're coming up on the last sighting of the Arcwolves. It's time to get to work." Abe and Ellie smiled at each other.

They all helped lay the charges, picking their way over the rubble that covered the one straggling Arcwolf. Reginald said they would leave the body as evidence of the success of their mission. "For camera crews, the unearthing of an Arcwolf corpse is pure ratings gold. We'll let them do the lifting with their new excavators."

Once the charges were laid, the hovers made their way to where Sophie had broken into the sewers just a few abandoned streets away from the sha sector barracks.

It felt strange to Abe to see the familiar landscape from this side. To him it seemed much smaller, full of paranoid people angry at a huge, uncaring city that had largely forgotten they existed. The Frees of the sha sector lived in fear of a takeover by Central, which had now dwindled to a single employee struggling for his own existence.

The excavator was very effective at tearing its way down into the street bed. Two dozen individual drills rotated on a larger drill, and the combination tore downward while spindly legs supported Reginald in his tiny cabin.

Below the street, they dropped into the upper sewer system. Abe could walk hunched over, while Ellie could have stood upright if she hadn't been concerned about the moss and lichens on the walls and ceiling. Abe recognized several species he'd seen in the Wilds.

The excavator continued its descent for another few meters, tearing down into a lower sewer system below the first. This one smelled of old decay, more like a cave than anything man-made. It was taller, and Sophie said that it should connect with the other lower sewer pipes that dropped down far below the world city in the distance.

Following the excavator, they walked toward the Wilds until they came to a blockage. The entire sewer line was filled with a yellowish mass.

"I haven't seen this compound in ages!" Reginald came out of the excavator to prod the yellow. "It's an expanding glue. Some holdover from Beforer times, ancient tech. Expands like crazy, but is not very sturdy. Shouldn't be that hard to tear through it."

"According to the reports," said Sophie. "Ilya's grandfather blew up these tunnels, so be careful."

"No need to be careful," said Reginald. "We'll lay tunnel-bubble as we go. I'll anchor in that, just in case there's no pipe up ahead."

Ellie and Abe were on resupply duty, ferrying the pallets of tunnel-bubble forward as Reginald worked the excavator and Sophie fed him new canisters.

The sprayers of the excavator would send out little pulses of tunnel bubble every time the feet advanced. Soon Ellie and Abe were walking back down a long, greenish tunnel as the excavator went deeper and deeper.

Abe looked up. "Do you think we're below the barracks yet?"

"Nope," Ellie glanced at him with her headlamp, momentarily blinding him. "About fifteen more mets. Didn't you ever learn to sight-step measure? Free cadets practice it from the time we can walk. It lets you know where you are if you have to move in pitch black."

"No," Abe jingled his toolbelt. "'Cyclers have another solution for that. It's called a flashlight."

"Oh, smart," Ellie almost didn't sound sarcastic. "Papa would drill us in the pitch black. Get out of bed, find your clothes, and load your gun. All silently, in darkness."

Don't Frees all sleep with guns under their pillows?" Abe steered the pallet mini-hover over the lip of where the tunnel bubble ended.

"No, that's only fangirls," said Ellie. "The last thing you want to do is flail around half-awake with a loaded firearm. You're going to end up sweeping loved ones, maybe even firing on them before you've assessed the situation."

"What's to assess?" Abe climbed up the pile of rubble they'd kicked into a rough semblance of stairs leading to the upper sewer and the hovers. He reached down. Ellie took his hand even though she didn't need it. They both knew her balance was better than Abe's, but it was nice to let him think he was helping.

"Seriously, what's to assess?" Abe and Ellie pulled out another pallet of tunnel bubble and dropped it onto the mini-hover. "I thought the answer for Frees to every problem was guns. Shoot first, ask questions later."

"And yet you're still alive," Ellie pointed out. "Remember, just because you can do something doesn't mean you do. Having firearms around is like having fire extinguishers around. It's stupid not to have enough, and you make sure they're ready to hand. But you hope to never have to use them. Frees treat firearms like shovels. We're not paranoid about them like 'Cyclers." She adjusted the rifle on her back, suddenly conscious of something she simply wore unconsciously like a pair of pants.

Abe thought about it as they lowered the pallet into the lower tunnel. "So for you, guns are just like my toolbelt. But why do you have so many of them?"

Ellie shrugged. "Why do you have so many tools?"

"I have so many tools because they all have a specific purpose."

"Do you have more of any one tool?"

"Yeah, I have a lot of tools like hex keys, so I can replace them. Like, when I lost that hex key the night Scar was going to attack you."

"Oh, you mean the night I saved your butt."

"No, I mean the night you unnecessarily shot Scar when…"

"Shut up."

"No, I'm serious. He was just scouting…"

"No, I'm serious. Shut up. There's something moving up ahead." Ellie unslung her rifle as the mini-hover slowed to a stop. "See that? It doesn't like the light?"

Abe looked past her. There was a shadow up ahead, nearly to the new tunnel-bubble tunnel. It looked big in the light from their headlamps.

"Flip off your headlamp," said Ellie. "I want it to stop moving. I should be able to see it clearer on my scope." She hunched down over the pallet of tunnel-bubble canisters and flipped off her own lamp.

Abe resisted the urge to peer forward and flipped off his headlamp. The darkness blinded him and he reached out to the pallet of tunnel bubble to steady himself. "Is it an Arcwolf?" His voice was suddenly hushed like the darkness had wrapped around his throat.

"No," said Ellie. "It looks…human. But it's not. A Wanderer? But there's something wrong with him."

"Let me see," Abe felt the hairs on the back of his neck rise. The other 'Cycler kids had told him stories about plaguers, Wanderers coming out of the Wilds that got infected with some ancient Beforer disease and had to be put down before they could spread it. How could a plaguer have gotten down into the tunnels?

"You're holding it wrong," Ellie fussed. "Hold it steady. You already broke one of my sights this year."

Abe ignored her and focused on the figure. It wasn't a Wanderer. Even distorted through the infrared sight the shape was wrong. The arms were too long, the legs too short, and the head was too large. Abe whistled. As the creature turned, he saw the infrared go white around the creature's mouth.

"Do you have a death wish?" Ellie pulled her rifle away from him. "Are you trying to tell the Arcwolves we're down here?"

"I had to get its attention," explained Abe. "I needed to see its mouth to be sure it's a shambler."

"A shambler," Ellie couldn't hide her disbelief. "Those aren't real. They're like plaguers, made-up monsters to scare little cadets."

"No, they're real," said Abe. "Not everyone left the Wilds in time. During the end of the Corporate Wars, a lot of people risked the Wilds rather than give up to Dubsee. Some of them came out at the end of the wars, but some of them stayed. All the Wanderers that have gone in since then, not all of them died. A few came out with terrible cancers and stories about other people who still lived in caves. Shamblers are just the terribly sick Wanderer children."

"What's wrong with their mouths?"

"They drink radioactive water. The radiation burns them out from inside. So their mouths are very hot. Supposedly they glow in the dark."

"You're saying that a really radioactive Wanderer kid is up there? A real-life shambler headed for your mom?"

Abe nodded, then realized Ellie couldn't see him. "Yeah."

"Then I think that's one less Wanderer kid," Ellie cocked her rifle. Abe had to agree. The shamblers were better off dead.

Something collided with the mini-hover, slamming it into Ellie and Abe. Abe went over the handle and spilled off the side, grabbing at the pallet and coming away with a canister of tunnel bubble as he sprawled on the ground.

Abe shook his head and heard Ellie gasping. He struggled to his feet and ran into the mini-hover that had been pushed to the side. Cursing, Abe limped around in the darkness until he remembered he had a headlamp. He flipped it on and something hissed on the other side of the mini-hover. Looking, Abe saw a hunched form.

It wasn't clothed, but its skin was rough and scaly like bark. Odd growths jutted from its back and head. The arms were mottled and the hands that grasped Ellie's throat were long and spidery.

Ellie was struggling, but her legs were trapped under the mini-hover. She smashed her fist into the creature's face, but it seemed to be so swollen that her fists sank in rather than striking bone.

Abe hefted the tunnel-bubble canister and threw it at the creature's head. It bounced off, but the creature turned its ruined face toward Abe even as it tightened its grip on Ellie.

"Draw it, Ellie! Draw in the radiation!" Abe reached for another canister.

Ellie gripped the creature's arms and stared at it. The creature howled, the terrible lowing sound of an animal in pain. Now it was lifting Ellie, dragging her out from under the mini-hover. But then Abe saw it was Ellie holding on to the creature, digging her fingers into its swollen limbs. She had a look of hunger on her face, a fierce joy even as she struggled for breath.

The creature swung Ellie around and flung her at Abe. To Abe's own surprise he caught her and they didn't fall.

Swinging its head from side to side, the creature eyed them. A mass grew over most of one of its eyes and pushed what Abe supposed must be a nose off one side of its face. The creature picked up the canister Abe had thrown, holding it as if it had no weight. Then the creature turned toward the new tunnel and took off at a loping gait.

"Down," Ellie gasped. Abe didn't have time to drop her. She rolled out of his arms, grabbed up her rifle, and sighted on the creature.

A shot reverberated along the tunnel. The creature didn't pause.

"Damn resilient, radioactive…" Ellie put a new bullet into the chamber.

"Hit the canister!" Abe called to her.

"You sure?" Ellie was already sighting.

"Yes, cement firework," Abe remembered what Reginald had said.

The second shot was followed by a ka-whump, less an explosion and more the sound of hard mud hitting pavement.

Ellie sighted. 'That's a mess." She let Abe peer through her scope.

"Yikes," he grimaced. "That's a horrible sculpture. Poor shambler."

"Better poor shambler than poor mom," said Ellie. "Can we still get the mini hover around it?"

"I think so," said Abe.

The mini-hover scraped the edge of the tunnel-bubble explosion that held the trapped shambler in an eternity of frozen running. Ellie kicked at it, but it was so hard her boot just bounced off.

25 CAVE IN

Ellie

Ellie couldn't see the excavator, which didn't bother her. Maybe the tunnel had turned. By her reckoning, they were under the barracks of sha sector now, and the tunnel ahead stretched under the courtyard for training Free cadets.

Only when they came to the end of the tunnel and only saw Sophie with the last pallet of tunnel bubble did Ellie get concerned. Abe was already moving forward, but his increase in speed was always gradual, like he was picking up steam. Ellie matched him easily, her long stride matching his own.

Abe was still pushing the mini-hover, but Ellie shoved it to the side. They ran together to where Sophie stood.

Below Sophie was a great hole, dropping down into the blackness beyond their headlamps.

"He just disappeared," Sophie's voice was flat. "The excavator accelerated when it hit open space, and he hadn't put in the anchor. He went down before he could brake."

Abe stared downward. "It looks like there might be something down there."

"If we'd only gotten a bit further," said Sophie. "I think the Wilds start just on the other side of this hole."

"No, said Ellie. "That's the start of the wall. But I doubt there are any more holes like this one under the wall. It would collapse." She peered down at the hole, then unslung her rifle and aimed down into the hole. Through the scope, she could see a small shape moving. "He's not dead, and I think the excavator is climbing, but it's clunky. I think it keeps slipping. Watch it!" She ducked backward as the spiked anchor hook shot past them and buried itself in the roof of the tunnel. It started to strain as it took weight, then tore free of the roof.

"Catch it!" Abe grabbed Ellie and pushed her rifle under the falling hook.

Ellie fought the urge to let the hook fall rather than let it scrape down her rifle. She could see the scratches all along the rifle, but Abe caught the hook and thrust it into a slight depression in the tunnel floor. The sharp edge of the hook caught and dug into the tunnel bubble, where it stuck fast.

There was a long pause, then they heard a whining sound as the excavator slowly rewound its anchor hook, slowly pulling itself upward.

Grinding, the excavator slowly climbed into view. All of them cheered. Two of its legs were broken, shredded metal showing how Reginald had slowed his descent. Reginald was bloody but smiled and waved as he came into view. Instead of returning to the same side of the tunnel, Reginald crawled along the edge until he found purchase on the far side with the remaining legs. He brought the drill back into motion and continued drilling on the far side as if nothing had happened.

Perched beyond the hole the excavator only dug for another minute before it broke through. The tunnel beyond was thick with roots and white vines. Instead of stopping, Roderick continued drilling until there was a spray of torn roots and vines behind him.

When Roderick stopped he backed the excavator up to the edge of the hole. He got out and unwound a long hose from the back of the excavator. Walking to the edge of the hole, Roderick began spraying tunnel-bubble in quick bursts. He threw handfuls of roots into the spray so that the tunnel bubble gradually extended out over the hole. Soon Roderick was standing in space, fearlessly throwing and spraying as he went. Ellie, Abe, and Sophie moved forward as Roderick finished the narrow bridge he'd made and firmed up his connection to the near side of the hole. They fed Roderick new canisters and he made the walk back and forth, replenishing the excavator. Then he waved them all back and got into the excavator.

Roderick used the drill to widen the tunnel's mouth on his side, slowly allowing him to turn around. Several large roots seemed enraged by this action, tearing themselves loose and smacking the excavator's dented sides.

Starting back toward them, the excavator began secreting tunnel bubble, finishing the tunnel. As the excavator reached the side of the hole, Ellie found herself holding her breath and took Abe's hand. He glanced over at her. "It has more than sufficient tensile strength. But I'm worried about his driving."

"Whatever," Ellie grinned at him. "You're as scared as I am."

"Yeah," Abe admitted.

The excavator crawled along the narrow bridge, secreting the tunnel bubble in an ever-thickening layer in front of it. To Ellie, it felt like ten minutes before the excavator touched down on their side. They had to move back while Roderick finished the connection to the existing tunnel bubble.

Roderick got out and skirted around the edge of the excavator to stand with them. "That's it," he shrugged.

"Amazing work!" Said Abe.

"Thanks," said Roderick. "I kept kicking myself for not keeping that anchor in every time I moved forward. I was warned."

"We're not quite done," said Sophie. "The Arcwolves will be suspicious of the bridge. It will sound odd and unsafe to them. We need something to lure them across."

Abe looked over at Ellie. "Something like Skullron carcasses?"

Sophie nodded. "I don't know where we'd get those...wait, Ellie, don't you have a bag of dead Skullron?"

Ellie blushed. "Yeah. I'm not using it anymore."

Roderick shook his head. "The ways of you border people are strange indeed. Let's head back to the hovers and bring in your bag of dead Skullron. Now that you're not using them for whatever you use dead Skullron for, and no, I don't want to know. The ways of the border are too strange for us poor city dwellers."

As they returned down the tunnel, they came upon the shambler, frozen in its cocoon of tunnel bubble. Sophie was horrified and hurried them past as if the shambler was still dangerous. Roderick used the excavator to push both the shambler and its cocoon back, then dug into the tunnel wall beyond the tunnel bubble to bury the two of them in the wall forever. They disappeared behind a spray of tunnel bubble.

Back on the surface, Ellie got her sack of Skullron. Before Sophie could object, Ellie and Abe headed back down into the tunnel.

Ellie could only see the bridge as a slight elevation in the tunnel floor until they stepped out onto the hollow surface. Abe's boots sounded like rocks hitting the tunnel-bubble surface.

"Those are crazy loud boots," Ellie turned to him.

"Better than being sneaky," Abe shrugged.

"Oh, you're the opposite of sneaky," Ellie assured him.

Abe bent forward to kiss her. Ellie responded with a quick peck, then emptied her sack of dead Skullron on the bridge.

"Wow," said Abe. "Nothing like a pile of dead Skullron to set the mood. Don't look, Cyrano. I hope none of your relatives are in here." He shifted the Skullron around with his boots, then picked up a few and placed them at various points along the bridge.

Ellie sniffed. "Dead Skullron smell sort of like that fake fish they serve in mess."

"Thanks," said Abe. Now I'll never eat that fish again." He stomped past her.

"Are you mad?" Ellie caught up with him.

"Kind of," Abe looked back at the bridge behind them. "It's hard enough to be brave enough to try and kiss you without a pile of Skullrons getting involved."

"Am I that scary?"

"Super macho killer Free girl who can suck radiation? Yeah, you're pretty scary." Abe blinded her momentarily with his headlamp as he looked at her.

"I know. But beyond that, am I scary?"

"Isn't that enough?"

"You know what I mean."

Abe thought. "Do you mean do I still want to kiss you? Yeah, I always want to kiss you. It's just been a death wish for so many years it's kind of hard to remind myself I won't necessarily be beaten bloody if I try."

Ellie grabbed his shoulder and kissed him. She realized she had to stretch up onto her tiptoes to reach his lips. "You're taller than me," she said with surprise.

Abe shrugged. "Yeah, only usually I slump over so much you can't tell."

"Don't slump," said Ellie.

"You sound like my mother."

"You look sexy when you don't slump."

"You still sound like my mother." Ellie recoiled and slapped at him. Abe smiled. "Just joking."

Ellie punched his arm, or she would have. Abe swiveled out of her way and caught her arm in a wrist lock.

"Nice," Ellie complimented him. "But I was just being affectionate."

"Oh, is that what Frees have been doing to me all these years? Showing me affection?"

"That's true," Ellie sobered. "You'll have to face Todd at some point. I'll have to show you his weaknesses."

"Todd has weaknesses? I thought he was a killing machine."

"Oh, he is." Ellie nodded. "But he's predictable. And he's so strong he hasn't bothered to get fast. A slow, overconfident killing machine."

"Great," Abe sighed. "I'm so liking my chances. Killing machine vs. fainting boy."

"You're not a fainter anymore. But he won't be expecting any resistance from you."

"So I'll just put up enough resistance to piss him off."

"No, you need to surprise him and knock him out before he overpowers you."

"I'm sure you've got a plan."

"Not yet. I have to think about your strengths."

Abe looked at his arms. "That shouldn't take too long."

They were distracted by each other as they climbed out of the tunnel into pulsing lights. Above them hung two dozen hovers, all bearing world city security logos in dancing red neon colors.

26 REALLY CAUGHT

Abe

"Ah, there they are," said Roderick. He was talking to three grim-looking people with world city security uniforms festooned with glittering rank badges. "Our young heroes who reported the stray Arcwolf. Isn't that right?" He walked them over and gripped them both by the shoulders. "They just put down a trap of poisoned Skullron corpses in case another one ever escapes."

"Do you think that's likely?" The woman who spoke looked like Roderick if someone had dehydrated Roderick, given him heavy long hair, and put him on stilts. The skin hung off her face in thin folds that couldn't truly be called jowls. She peered down at Abe and Ellie as if her red-rimmed eyes could see into their bones.

"Not at all likely, Ms. Brone, ma'am," Roderick continued. "As you already know, I blew up the one Arcwolf they reported."

"The border report we intercepted at world city intelligence was very alarming. I want no alarming things to be reported in the coming weeks. As you know, I'm due for a new liver. Out for at least three days, they tell me."

"Ah, yes," Roderick nodded. "An important Three like yourself will be missed."

Commander Brone smiled without humor. "I fully expect my subordinates to sabotage me while I'm gone. So I'm dealing with this first." She waved her hand at the hole. "Fill this in. I'll start these hovers on a bombing run of the Wilds."

Sophie gasped. "You can't!"

Commander Brone turned to her. "Actually, I can. It's well within my jurisdiction as head of the energy division of our little planet. You're just lucky I was in the area."

"But we've estimated that it will cause increased growth…"

"Ah, a true 'Cycler. Good for you, dear. Your estimates are always highly suspect. 'Cyclers have a fixation on the relative merits of that radioactive wasteland. Surface bombing will thin the Arcwolf packs without destabilizing any of the deeper radioactive deposits. We'll make sure to avoid direct hits on the thermal lines in any sector."

"But what if there is regrowth?"

Commander Brone turned to Sophie, who suddenly seemed very short. "If there is growth, then we will bomb more. Bombing looks good. It's the definition of taking action. Besides, I've been looking for an excuse to use the cluster bombs I ordered a few years back. You don't want bombs to get rusty and old. They aren't as efficient."

Sophie wanted to argue, but Commander Brone held up her palm and flipped on an array of embedded communications equipment that lit up her lined face with a sickly yellow and red glow. "You can begin your initial runs. Target carefully in the areas near the border walls. I want a ring of fire around that whole mess by tomorrow. If I can't see it from space, you haven't done enough."

Sophie was pale. "But the Arcwolves…"

"Fear not," Commander Brone smiled thinly. "The Arcwolves will be bombed well back from the border walls. They'll retreat into the depths of the Wilds. There's nothing to worry yourself over."

"Right you are, ma'am," Roderick clicked his heels. "I'll get right on this, then."

"Yes, carry on," Brone waved at him. "Oh, on my way here I noticed your superior Four has been freezing you out. Funny, I only saw competence in your reports. So I took a moment to override his security clearance and found your deleted report on his embezzling. He'll be on his way to the asteroid belt tomorrow. Congratulations. You're now in charge. They say Sixes run the world city, but I'm afraid you'll have to make do with being a Four. I'm sure you'll figure out what to do with the increased salary and housing allowance. Your boss had a very nice penthouse on the 329th floor. Just above the cloud line. We should all experience a sunset once in our lives, don't you think?." Commander Brone smiled thinly again. "Now I must go," she coughed. "Being in liver failure is so inconvenient to getting my work done. Carry on, Commander."

"Thank you, ma'am!" Roderick beamed. The gaunt Three shuffled back to her personal hover and took off. In a mass, the other hovers lifted and moved toward the border wall.

"We have to warn all the Arcwolves," Sophie was beside herself.

Abe remembered all the different screens in Uncle Gabriel's lab. "Uncle Gabriel has an early warning system. If there's anything that can be done, he'll do it." Abe told his mom.

Roderick was already spraying the edge of the tunnel hole with the excavator and humming to himself.

"Well, I'm glad you're happy," Sophie turned to him.

"As you should be," said Roderick. "I intend to reclassify this area as moderately radioactive and possibly relabel nearby sewer pipes as being hot thermals. So any and all 'Arcwolf sightings' in this area will be assumed to be a scanner error."

"But all the Arcwolves in the Wilds…" Sophie looked toward the hovers already spreading along the edge of the Wilds to begin their bombing.

"There's nothing we can do," said Roderick. "Superior Commander Brone has to do something drastic to keep her position. She knows she'll be blamed. Even with the bombing, she's going to be hard-pressed not to end up on the belt herself. Letting me be underfunded will be all her fault. Speaking of which, I have to fill this hole and then head back to the office to steal and promote an office staff for myself. You know anyone looking for work?"

"We might," said Abe. "It depends on what happens when the bombs start to fall."

Ellie

The bombing of the edge of the Wilds was carried out with a precision that only world city bureaucracy could manage. Abe, Ellie, and Sophie returned to a subdued and troubled sha sector. The Frees were mourning two dead of their own. One had been a young cadet who'd fallen and struck his head when the Arcwolves ran through the line. The other had been a Free retired soldier who had joined the line and suffered a stroke as the Arcwolves advanced. The Arcwolves, for all their terrible reputation, had killed none of the Frees. They had stolen rifles, tearing them from the Free's hands and injuring Frees who fought them. The behavior baffled the Frees, who'd been prepared to die. Ellie heard more than one of them complain about unnatural behavior. "I had my knife, and it had me on the ground. It got cut, but it let me go." It kept hold of my rifle, like it knew what a rifle could do, even when I was punching it." "Had me by the throat, but eased up. Look, you can barely see the teeth marks."

Abe told Ellie the 'Cyclers were more concerned about the thermal pipes. But they had been assured that the bombing would be all surface. Sha sector had been the first to be bombed, and Ellie had barely felt the explosions. These cluster bombs were meant to touch down lightly, then shred anything around them.

Sophie and Franklin were busy working with the other 'Cyclers along the line calculating a possible catastrophic response from the vegetation. Abe said it was basically that the Wilds could respond to the threat to its growth by growing larger and faster. "It's like if you tear up ground in the courtyard," he pointed to where they were walking. "The new empty soil means the fastest-growing plants have an advantage. Think about that happening, but way faster out in the Wilds. Only the fastest, most rapidly growing plants already survive out there."

Abe and Ellie were looking up at the newly installed automatic gun towers. The old ones had been dismantled and the new ones installed immediately before the news of an Arcwolf sighting was made public. For a day after the announcement, the sky above the sha sector had been full of camera drones. But Superior Commander Brone had cleaned things up to a point where there was nothing camera-worthy. None of the boundary folk would speak to reporters. Sophie tried to get her concerns about the plants heard, but no one wanted a story about possible plant growth in a time of increased Arcwolf threat. Sophie never mentioned anything that could be considered "pro-Arcwolf." She knew better.

Within hours, the preliminary boundary bombing was completed. Superior Commander Brone reassured everyone that the border was safe. About that time Free patrols along the border started reporting vines breaking through along the border wall. They were growing fast enough that you could watch them crack the ancient cement, pushing through like reddish-brown fingers.

Superior Commander Brone was paying attention. The increased growth meant that the Arcwolf habitat was rebuilding along the wall too fast for the news to have forgotten the threat. She warned all border inhabitants inside while dozens of hovers laden with burn materials torched the plants along the border.

For three days, they continued the burns. For a few days afterward, the smoldering ashes stayed quiet. It seemed to have worked. Ellie worked on border patrol and Abe was busy teaching his dad about Gabriel's null suit. The 'Cyclers were already planning to send a mission to see Gabriel's Wilds lab as soon as Ilya gave them permission.

Ellie hadn't decided to join the mission yet. Part of her was afraid once she went into the Wilds she wouldn't want to come back. Ellie spent a lot of her time hungry for radiation along the border. She'd had to visit the radiation ward the day before. An old 'Cycler made a miraculous recovery after Ellie left.

Walking along the border, Ellie felt the warmth beneath her feet. Ed, her patrol partner, looked at her strangely when Ellie knelt and felt the ground. "Something's running under here," Ellie told him. "I think the plants are going under us."

Ed looked at the wall, still blackened by the days of hover torching. He shook his head. "There's nothing growing anywhere near the wall."

"I know," said Ellie. "There's something growing under it."

"So it's not our problem," Ed shrugged. "Who cares if the roots grow under? It's not like they're dangerous."

Ellie looked at the edge of the barracks beyond where she felt the warmth. A long crack ran through the cement. It looked new, but there were already reddish-green sprouts pushing up through the holes.

"You're probably right," said Ellie. "But do you mind if I run down this crack for a bit? Just take me a minute."

"Sure. Knock yourself out," yawned Ed. "There haven't been any Arcwolf sightings in days." Ed shifted his rifle to his other shoulder.

Ellie stalked above the crack until she got past the barracks. The crack ran straight away from the border wall like the spoke of a wheel. As Ellie followed it, she saw it run straight under the buildings of the Alienation Zone. As she looked left and right, Ellie saw similar cracks along the surface every few mets. In some places, she could already see the stubby bumps of vines pushing their way up through the new holes.

After her shift, Ellie went to see Papa.

Ilya had no time for his daughter's root cracks. "There are roots, there are cracks. The Alienation Zone is old. What do you think? When things get old, they crack. Roots grow. What are you talking about?"

"No Papa, these roots are growing really fast."

"If they grow fast, we burn them back. Let me know when they grow faster than we can burn them. Then I'll be worried.

"Right now, I've got this new Four Roderick trying to hire away my Free linemen. He's offering benefits and employee status. Of all the underhanded tricks!"

"Papa, you need to do something."

"You sound just like that mom of your boyfriend. She was here earlier with charts and graphs. She's been stirring up trouble all along the line, getting other sectors riled up. Epsilon and Jota are taking weed cutters out with them on patrol. Can you imagine? Linemen doing gardening. Ridiculous!"

Ellie saw the anger in his face and realized she'd get nowhere with him now. She left him fuming and went looking for Abe. Abe always made her feel better.

Abe was finishing a talk on mitochondrial care and feeding to a group of rapt 'Cyclers. Ellie waited while they shook his hand and asked him technical questions about solute levels and ultraviolet exposure. When he was finished, Abe grinned at her.

"Hey, miss me that much? Here to fool around with the professor?" He wiggled his eyebrows at her and laughed.

Ellie grabbed him and leaned into him. "Maybe."

"Oh, wow," Abe blushed. "I was just kidding. I'm still not used to you liking me."

"You were fine with it when we were out in the Wilds," Ellie pointed out.

"Yeah, but it's different here. I'm back to being a geek. I keep waiting for your dad to come to punch me out."

"He's too busy trying to keep his linemen from defecting to Central." Ellie poked at Abe's presentation slurry. "Arcwolf blood?"

"Just a synthetic version. It won't be as good, but it gives us practice. Maybe one of us can figure out a way to keep the little guys active."

"Oh, speaking of keeping things active, I came up with a combat combination that might work against Todd."

"Really?"

"Sure. It starts with you fainting as soon as he punches you."

"That I can do."

"You got a minute?"

"Sure. I'll probably regret it though."

Twelve takedowns later, Abe understood what Ellie was doing. It only took him five tries to do the same to her.

"Nice!" Ellie slapped Abe on the shoulder. He bent clumsily toward her and she kissed him.

"Better," Ellie smiled. "We'll have to practice that some more until you get   it   right."

"I'll practice on my own," Abe started kissing his own wrist.

"Kind of adorable and …kind of creepy," Ellie pushed herself up.

Abe caught her around the waist and picked her off the floor. "Have you lost weight?"

Ellie smiled. "No, you've got a little muscle now. From all that Arcwolf wrestling."

"Hey," Abe got serious and put her down. "Are you doing OK with your radiation hunger?"

Ellie looked away. "I visit the radiation ward. It helps."

"We've got to get you back out there. In the Wilds, you'd never have to worry."

Ellie looked at him. "But you can't live there."

"Sure I can. I'll wear a null suit."

"But you could have an accident, tear a hole in your suit." Ellie's gut twisted.

"I'll be fine if you're around to kiss it and make it better."

"Well, I guess that's good because the Wilds are growing. I saw vines on the other side of the barracks."

"Really?" Abe looked shocked. "I've seen the calculations, but I think that exceeds the estimates...by a lot."

"Come see for yourself."

27 REGROWTH

Abe

It was hard for Abe to focus on the threat of the stubby vines when Ellie's hand was warm in his own. He was surprised that his hand was bigger than hers. Fatter anyway. Ellie's fingers were longer than his, but when he gripped her hand Abe felt bigger and more protective.

They walked together to see the extent of the growth, but the cracks disappeared under the abandoned buildings of the Alienation Zone. More out of wanting to just walk with Ellie, Abe suggested they go up to the next major abandoned street, picking their way through the older broken pavement as they walked. He noticed little spouts of the vines appearing everywhere.

"They must seed from any fragment," Abe mused, mostly to himself.

"You mean every time we blow them up, we spread them?"

"Yeah. Those bombing runs were the best thing for spreading the Wilds."

At the next street crossing, and the one after that, the fresh rupture of the thick vines was visible.

Ellie bent down to the fresh cracks and put in her fingers.

"What are you doing?" Abe felt the short hairs on the back of his neck prickle. Was his girlfriend taking a radiation drink?

"I'm just checking," said Ellie, standing up. "These are just as warm as the roots near the barracks. The vines are spreading radiation, pulling it along with them."

"That's bad," Abe looked out over the Alienation Zone toward the two-milers in the distance. "But I don't think anyone in energy production is going to care about a few stray plants."

Ellie

Abe was wrong. But wasn't the energy department that cared. It was an alert from food production that made the Dubsee higher-ups go crazy. One tiny sprout, born much farther than the others by a strong southern wind, navigated the extensive filtration system and landed in the lower solar fields of Bela-10585, the nearest two-miler. An inspecting Sixer found the sprout and checked it for radiation levels. They were well above the limit, triggering an inspection of the filtration system. It was infested with bits of the plant and spores, requiring extensive, expensive replacements. The Five in charge of the replacements went looking for someone else to blame for his budget overrun and started asking questions about the recent Wilds bombing runs. What she found she brought to her Four. He called over to Energy production with a bill and a demand that Energy Production reimburse Food Production for the replacement of all nearby two-miler filtration systems. When Energy Production squawked and said they wouldn't pay, the Four in charge cited ancient research from the original attempts to bulldoze the Wilds. The resulting expansion of the radioactive plant material had resulted in the evacuation and designation of the Alienation Zone as a buffer against future plant growth.

An investigation carried out with extreme robotic efficiency backed by hundreds of satellite images showed the current bombing and burning of the Wilds plant matter had aerosolized large enough quantities of radioactive material that the existing Alienation Zone was now contaminated to a point where the current border wall had been completely overrun.

Dubsee informed the border wall population that the heightened levels of radioactive materials made it a death sentence to remain along the existing border wall. A new border wall had to be built, and it was questionable if the nearest two-miler, Bela-10585, would be habitable going forward. The extraordinary debacle cost Superior Commander Brone her position, but she was able to stay on the planet, pleading medical issues with her liver transplant. The border wall was ordered evacuated. Orders came down from Central to abandon the wall. No one expected Dubsee to move so fast.

"They want us to retreat," Ellie could see Ilya was beside himself. "Frees never retreat. We're not going anywhere."

"There isn't a border here anymore, sir," The uncomfortable Central messenger was standing at attention in Ilya's rebuilt control room.

"What about the 'Cyclers? Are they pulling out?" Ilya gestured down to the new 'Cycler excavators ringing the central square of the sha sector.

"I believe the 'Cyclers have arranged to stay behind to lengthen the existing thermal energy system through the alienation zone out to the new border wall."

"What about our border wall? Why don't they just repair our wall? We've been asking for that for ages."

"Sorry, sir. The new approved wall goes ten mets up and ten mets down. It has a fine mesh that catches spores another sixty mets above the wall. It will be a technical marvel, consuming a full percentage of all Dubsee's output this fiscal year. Our experts say it will be deep enough to stop the root systems from getting past into the world city."

Ilya grunted. "And they want us to man this new wall?"

"Not necessary, sir. Fully automated."

"Right, because that's worked so well before. So what's going to happen to the Frees?"

The messenger looked at his feet. "I believe asteroid mining was mentioned, sir. Not being employees, line guards are not really eligible for lateral transfers. I'm sure you understand…"

"Get out," Ilya turned away. He rubbed his face and glared at Ellie, who'd been listening at attention. "Your boyfriend gets to stay, but we're all going to get shipped off to the belt like criminals."

Ellie stared at him. "Now do you want me to finally ask him?"

Ilya threw up his hands. "Sure, sure. See if your 'Cycler boy can figure a way out of this one."

28 A NEW ALLIANCE

Abe

It wasn't as impossible a problem as it could have been. Abe explained to his fellow 'Cyclers the sheer amount of physical work necessary to build and maintain a thermal system through the expanding Wilds. They soon recognized the work was beyond the existing 'Cyclers, even with the newest excavators. So construction crews were necessary. But employees skilled at construction could receive far more credits and far less radiation off-world. That left the Frees as the only willing workforce. So the choice was between accepting a work shortfall that might jeopardize the 'Cyclers ability to stay in the Wilds or accepting the Frees as coworkers.

For the Frees, it was shifting from rifles to scanners and from walking patrols to traveling by excavator. Instead of Arcwolf sightings, they would report and patch thermal leaks. Now that the existing wall was was no longer considered a real barrier, excavators were venturing out into the original Wilds. Abe's new null suits were strong enough to withstand short exposures to higher radiation. Abe used plant mitochondria from the now ubiquitous Wild vines to populate his suits. They weren't as good as Uncle Gabriel's suits, but they were a great improvement on anything Franklin had been able to do. But Abe and Sophie still planned to secretly introduce the Arcwolf packs to the settlers once the new society living inside the new wall got settled.

While Abe was keeping both Frees and 'Cyclers from getting radiation burns, Ellie was busy dealing with them. She was unofficially part of the radiation ward staff, who said she had a "healing presence" for their worst cases. As her healing workload increased, Ellie had refused to stay cooped up inside the ward, so they brought patients up to her on the watchtower bundled on stretchers. She would sit next to patients for a time, both of them staring out of her watchtower at the sea of greens and browns of the Wilds. When they came back, patients were much better.

In her non-healing time, Ellie was on patrol. She roamed all over the sha sector, which now included a huge chunk of the former Alienation Zone. Ellie mapped the major vines by touch, which made running the thermal lines alongside them much easier.

Abe still planned to go back into the Wilds to visit Uncle Gabriel. But one morning Uncle Gabriel and three Arcwolves came through the newly opened gates of what had been the old Wilds. The Arcwolves were pulling Uncle Gabriel on a makeshift sled. Uncle Gabriel was waving a white flag.

After a tense standoff, Ilya sent for Abe.

"Your uncle wants to speak to you," Ilya glowered at the old man on the sled.

"Uncle Gabriel!" Abe was surprised to see the old man looking so ill. "What are you doing here? It looks like you need another radiation bath."

"T-too many b-baths, Little Abe," Uncle Gabriel smiled up at him. "C-can't keep y-your body alive f-forever with m-mitochrondria. B-breaking down. I w-want to s-see my b-brother."

Abe got one of the Free guards to go get Franklin from the expanded workshop. Franklin had been perfecting a new flap design on the null suits and came out blinking into the bright sun of the courtyard. "What is it, Abe? Please tell me it's relevant to the current task at hand."

"I think so," said Abe. "You can ask a fellow inventor about your flap design."

"Gabriel?" Franklin rubbed his eyes. "They told me you were still alive. I had a hard time believing it."

Gabriel reached out his arms. "F-franklin, my brother, you look so g-good."

"Well, nobody shot me," Franklin bent low to hold his brother. "You're so thin. There can't be much food out there in the Wilds. We've got food here, plenty of food. Let me get you some."

"F-franklin," Uncle Gabriel clenched his brother's arm with his surprising strength. "I-I'm dying. I c-came to tell you h-how s-sorry I am."

"Sorry for going missing and never telling me you were alive?"

"F-for that t-too. But m-mostly sorry for t-taking your childhood," Gabriel grimaced and his body arched on the sled. "E-every day I w-went to school wh-while you st-stayed home. I f-felt so b-bad. If I c-could have, I w-would have t-traded with y-you."

Franklin looked at him. "I thought you loved going to school."

"N-no, I hated it. I h-had to pretend f-for our p-parents. I w-wanted to s-stay with y-you."

"I wish you could have stayed with me too," Franklin's eyes were suddenly full of tears. Abe, watching the two of them, was suddenly embarrassed and envious of the intense bond his dad and his uncle shared.

Uncle Gabriel said nothing more. His grip on his brother's arm gradually released, and he settled back on the makeshift sled. Abe knew he was dead before Franklin realized his brother had gone. With a wail, Franklin collapsed across his brother, crushing the now wilted flowers protruding from Uncle Gabriel's belly.

They buried Uncle Gabriel in a 'Cycler's grave, fully 'Cycled in six months into fertilizer. Though with that much radiation, Franklin said they would have to spread the fertilizer back into the Wilds.

Abe released the Arcwolves who had come with Uncle Gabriel, but they stayed around the barracks. After he caught several Free guards feeding them, Ilya promised to shoot them. Abe told them to go back to Scar. They left and did not return.

The proliferation of the vine sprouts led to a bumper crop of Skullron. With the continued absence of the Arcwolves, the Skullrons overran the border area, nesting beyond it in the Alienation Zone. Soon after other small creatures followed, shy beasts with odd faces who lived in holes high in the trees of the Wilds. These took to the rooftops of the Alienation Zone, and could be seen peering down while munching young vine shoots.

So many animals could not be maintained by roots alone. They got into the food stores. The other sectors, suffering from radiation and hunger, began to close down. 'Cyclers were heading back into the city, the Frees were going off-world to the asteroid belts. Only the sha sector resisted, its ranks swelling as hopeful holdouts flooded in from other sectors. But their addition made the food problem worse. Until the thermal lines were running, Dubsee seemed unwilling to extend any more credit for more food stocks.

After the fourth pantry raid by Skullron, Ilya tracked down Abe. "Call them, get them, do whatever you need to do! We can't kill the thieving Skullron fast enough to keep ourselves in food. Until the thermal pipes are completed, there are no more credits for food. We'll starve out here and end up eating nothing but Skullron poop. Call back those tame Arcwolves!"

Abe looked at him. "Even Scar?"

Ilya's face purpled. "Even Scar. We have a truce until the Skullrons are under control."

"No," said Abe. "I want you to end your war. The Arcwolves aren't the enemy anymore."

"Impossible! They're beasts, monsters…"

"Who can save our sector from starvation. We can't eat the radioactive Skullron, so all we'll have is their poop until the tunnels are completed."

"My head says no, my honor says no, but my stomach says yes." Ilya sighed. "It's foolish to die for revenge on a dumb beast. There is no honor in starving my people for the sake of a blood feud with an animal. I agree. The war is over. We no longer fight Arcwolves."

It wasn't a smooth transition. The first few times the Arcwolves appeared, every Free in the area had drawn on them. But over time, the reactions got less extreme. The Frees laughed when they saw Abe get shocked as he scratched behind the Arcwolves' ears. At first, it was just the youngest Arcwolves, the smallest. Scar stayed out of sight, hunting beyond the wall. But seeing Ellie playing with the Arcwolves, bounding around with them, brought more and more Frees into an agreement that the wolves weren't so bad. For their part, the Arcwolves loved Ellie, lying near her when they finished hunting for the day. She was practically part of the pack except for the one large female that Ellie continued to bribe with treats out of guilt for killing her baby.

Abe created an enclosure for the Arcwolves, something that could be publicly padlocked but secretly led down into the tunnel that Reginald and Sophie had made. The Frees felt safe, and the Arcwolves were free to roam out into the Wilds or down into the tunnels as they wished.

The new Four, Reginald, was zealous about the creation of the new border wall. It progressed with an efficiency only the great machines of Dubsee could bring. The same machines that could put a two-miler up in a month churned out a wall day and night. Soon the new border wall was complete.

But the combination of the Free work ethic and 'Cycler ingenuity was a match for the great machines. The thermal lines now ran out to the new wall, running easily alongside the vines that had softened the soil, shoving aside concrete and rock to find their way outward. It wasn't long before the thermal lines were hooked up, automated like the rest of the new wall.

Once their task was finished, the border folk of sha sector were given a choice. They would be allowed to live free in the "lost zone" or move beyond the wall. Reginald had worked some magic, so any and all of the border folk, Free or 'Cycler, could gain employee status. It meant that they could be lateral transfers, find work in the world city.

It was the perfect time for Abe to show off his new null suits. His barely tolerated Arcwolves had provided the needed mitochondria with their blood and Abe had three volunteers undergo extreme radiation exposure. When they emerged unscathed, the 'Cyclers of sha sector voted to become contractors of energy production, leaving world city employ. They were already mostly self-sufficient if they were willing to subsist on what the Wilds provided. But world city needed more energy sources and the Wilds had many untapped thermal lines. Once the 'Cyclers had new lines, they could sell energy to the world cities or use the surplus for themselves.

The Frees were struggling with being written out of work. Their border had been abandoned, their wall crumbling into ruin. They were guards without anything to guard. The new wall was automatic, run remotely by employees. While the Frees were offered other employment, many considered the option of working on the asteroid belt the only real alternative. After years on patrol, few considered working at some kind of desk as a job with any honor. Better to spend your days trying to eke out an existence surrounded by Wanderers and criminals. It was a life of trading ore for oxygen tanks and dehydrated food, but it would give the Frees the sense of an edge they couldn't find in the cattle pens or office cubicles of the world city.

Abe argued with his fellow 'Cyclers. No, they didn't absolutely need the Frees. It might be possible to get an employee workforce with high enough wages. But would that new workforce know which vines caused swollen rashes or that Skullrons loved stealing anything shiny? Allowing covers to rust, corrode and lose their shine before they were placed over sensitive connectors was second nature to Free and 'Cycler alike. The Frees had a knowledge of the Wilds that no amount of employee training would match. Abe was persuasive, and his status as a 'Cycler hero gave him great influence. The decision was made to offer the Frees employment, not as employees but on the same contract basis as before. Abe brought the offer to Ilya.

"Not interested," Ilya was packing the family things.

"You don't understand," Abe stood in the doorway. "It's the same deal you had before."

"Not the same deal. Now Frees work for 'Cyclers. Not equals. We lose all our freedom. Better off on the asteroid belt."

"Really?" Abe was losing his temper. "Better to go somewhere where no Free can ever fire another gun for fear of puncturing an air seal? Somewhere where your children grow up with the worst criminals? That's preferable to being our employees?"

Ilya looked at him. "Otherwise we retreat. Give up everything. Join the 'Cycler way of life. Grow my hair out in dreads." He rubbed the gray stubble on his head.

"What if you didn't have to change? What if we created a charter where Frees and 'Cyclers shared control?"

"Nice talk, but you know the 'Cyclers outthink the Frees. You'll make a tricky deal and hide it in the small print."

"What if it had to be simple? Simple language, simple contract. Any Free cadet could understand it."

"Why would the 'Cyclers do that? You know you have us over a barrel."

"We'd do it because there aren't enough of us to take care of all the pipelines in the other sectors, to explore, and to keep the energy production functioning. We need Frees to do the work you've been doing. Keeping things safe, making sure the repair trails stay clear, and yes even shooting the things that come out of the Wilds and try to eat us."

"So we would not be your employees? We are...partners?"

Abe made a face. "I can't speak for the other sectors. But in the sha sector, you're partners.

"The other sectors will pack up and go to the belt." Ilya waved his hand. "More for us to mine, yes? We will expand the sha sector up and down the old wall. Too dangerous for them to stay, but not too dangerous for us. We have my daughter, yes? She can take away radiation burns with a touch. What did you do to her, 'Cycler boy?"

Abe thought. "She's a human null suit."

Ilya laughed. "I see how hard that was for you. Cut through the big words and get to the meat of it. Maybe there's hope for you yet, 'Cycler boy."

"Maybe," Abe swallowed. "Sir, I'd like to buy your daughter a gun. With your permission, of course."

Ilya stopped. His fists tightened. His face started to get red. Then he took three long breaths and looked up at Abe. "What kind of gun? You know she's had her heart set on a pearl-handled .38 since she could talk."

Abe had been tensing for a blow, but took a breath himself. "Of course, sir. I know just the one."

Ilya looked at Abe. "You do, don't you? You will make her happy. If you don't, they will never find your body." He looked at Abe's ashen face. "What? It's traditional for a Free father to threaten his son-in-law. Part of the tradition, part of the fun. At some point in the ceremony, we have to arm wrestle. Don't worry, I'll let you win. But get to a shooting range. Even a drunken Free groom has to be able to hit a wine glass with a .22 at twenty mets. I suggest a big wine glass and sipping synthetic grape juice instead of wine until after that part. Don't worry about planning the ceremony. Gladys has been planning it out since the two of you came out of the Wilds. She's been hiding nice things in our backroom like a Skullron in nesting season. I imagine it will be quite a party."

29 MARRIAGE AND DEATH

Abe And Ellie

Abe and Ellie were married in a traditional Free ceremony on the second anniversary of their disappearance into the Wilds together. Gladys said that day had been the worst day of her life. Now that date would also be the happiest.

Abe finally presented Ellie with her pearl-handled .38, which she ignored, sweeping him into a full-body kiss that lasted through three coughing fits from Ilya.

Ellie gave Abe a snub-nosed .38 in a holster that hid the gun and perfectly matched his tool belt. Aware of the eyes on him, Abe swept her into an embrace that was equally passionate, if a little shorter than hers had been.

During the wineglass ritual, Abe's hand shook until Ellie put her arm around him in a loving way. She also tilted his aim the three degrees necessary for him to shatter the glass in spectacular fashion.

Franklin's contribution to the ceremony was completing paperwork for their civil union as contractors under World City Bela's laws. The paperwork entitled them to conceive one child, but that point was asterisked. The small print Franklin pointed out was that the one-child policy was being revisited for contractors within the new lost zone due to hazardous conditions it might be possible to have more.

Sophie gave them a surveillance tape for private viewing only. While that brought chuckles and bawdy jokes all around about their romantic escapades being caught on tape. But when Abe and Ellie viewed it later it only showed a stream of red pouring down a tunnel. Sophie panned out the camera to show the red stream was the Arcwolves returning to the Wilds through the tunnel they'd made.

It was after the ceremony, when Abe and Ellie were finally walking alone out in the courtyard, that Todd showed up. He didn't come alone. Three of his friends from the che sector flanked Ellie, forming a semi-circle with guns drawn.

"If she moves, shoot him," ordered Todd. "Don't do it, Ellie. Drop back or your 'Cycler gets it."

Ellie held up her hands. "I thought I smelled something bad. I should have known it was you, Todd."

"Too bad. I thought your nose was full of the stink from this 'Cycler garbage."

"Leave us alone, Todd. The old ways don't work anymore. Most of the Frees are leaving."

"I know. We ship out tomorrow for the belt. Most of the che sector has already left. But there's a little unfinished business I needed to take care of here first." Todd stepped toward Abe. "I guess a warning isn't enough, huh? Fat Abe the Mutie Lover? Too stupid to understand that you shouldn't touch Free girls? We need to make sure someone as stupid as you can't breed. Hold him." Todd gestured to one of his friends.

Ellie laughed. It was so unexpected even Abe turned toward her. "I never thought I'd see the day," Ellie laughed, "when big Todd would be so scared of a 'Cycler kid he'd ask for help. I'm surprised you didn't ask your mommy to come along. Wouldn't your Papa be proud?"

"Shut up," Todd pointed his knife at her. "I was only asking for help to go easy on your boy here. If he struggles, I might accidentally kill him."

Ellie laughed again. "Such a coward. Bring your boys because you're afraid of a girl. Ask for help because you're afraid of a 'Cycler."

"Don't drop your guard," Todd told his friends. "You remember how fast she is. Leave this fainting boy to me. C'mere, fattie, I've got a wedding gift for you. A ticket to the no-child plan. It's only going to hurt a lot."

Abe

Abe knew Ellie had bought him a chance. Just a chance. It was a long shot. Todd was armed. His friends had Ellie locked down. Abe couldn't even remember if Ellie was armed. She must be, right? Frees were always armed.

Todd grabbed Abe by the shoulder and Abe started to drop. Todd had been expecting this, and he reached forward to catch Abe with his other hand, the knife held loosely with two fingers and tilted away from Abe. Abe reached up quickly with both hands, twisting the knife sharply toward Todd. The wrist lock was painful. It was supposed to get Todd to drop the knife or let go with his other hand.

But Todd didn't follow the plan. Instead of letting go, he tightened his grip on the knife and Abe's shoulder. Abe's momentum carried him forward and on top of Todd as they fell backward together. The knife slid into Todd's chest just above his protective armor. Todd coughed, and blood came up. But as Abe struggled to rise, Todd gripped him even tighter. It was like a madness, forcing Abe down on top of him even as Todd stared into Abe's eyes. They grunted and strained, but Todd and Abe stayed locked together while Todd's mouth frothed blood. Abe watched as Todd's eyes lost focus. They still stared into his own. Abe lost himself in that murky, angry gaze.

Three cracks brought Abe back. He looked up. All three of Todd's friends were disarmed, holding hands and arms. Ellie had her smoking pearl-handled .38. They all stood in silence while the shots echoed and brought running footsteps.

Ilya and a crowd of late revelers came running up.

"What's going on here?" Ilya had his old rifle, worn in honor during the ceremony.

"Abe and Todd had a duel," Ellie spoke with authority.

"Oh, I'm so sorry," Ilya brushed his eyes. "Abe would have been a good husband. Where is his body?"

"Here," Abe disentangled himself from Todd. He had to rip his dress coveralls free of those clutching fingers.

"You...beat Todd?" Ilya looked around. "Ellie, did you shoot Todd first?"

"No," Ellie kept her eyes on Todd's three friends. "No one else got involved. Todd died honorably. Right, boys?"

Realizing that any other story would lead to a hearing, discipline, and possible expulsion as wanderers, the three men from che nodded.

Ilya looked at them all. "Well, since it was a fair fight, I see no reason for any investigation. Che sector will want to bury one of its own. We'll escort you back out of our sector to make sure there are no more...misunderstandings."

Ilya nodded to Abe. "I imagine this is first blood for you. It's an older Free tradition. Not one we practice much anymore. If it's done, it's usually to first blood, not to death. But it makes you a full Free man."

Abe responded by bending over and throwing up.

"Good man, can't handle his beer," Ilya told the crowd.

30 ENDING

Abe And Ellie

It wasn't happily ever after. No marriage is, and Ellie shared her father's difficulty with temper. The stresses of life got to them both. But Elle and Abe had learned to listen to each other's silences as well as their words. They lived as happy as some, and happier than most, in that new frontier of the lost zone.

Maybe it's easiest to talk about their first child, a Free 'Cycler, who could shoot and splice as soon as she could walk. Little Hope thought a toolbelt missing either a hex wrench or her trusty .22 was just not complete. She wore both for her workday alongside mom and dad.

"No, no," Abe reached out to catch his young daughter's hand. "Your laser sight is crooked."

"Tha-that's what y-you think," she had Ellie's nose. It was crinkled now with disdain for his ignorance. "I cor-corrected it for the ba-ballistic v-variation."

Abe fell silent. Beneath her childlike stutter she was so clever it scared even him. How could she not be with all of them teaching her everything they knew? She soaked it all in like a sponge, a thirsty root, like the radiation both she and her mom needed to survive.

"Hope? Hope, come in! It's time for your spotting practice! Stop bothering your father!" Ellie's voice called up the treehouse ladder.

"Y-yes, mommy!" Hope lit up, hugged Abe in his null suit, and threw herself through the opening, catching herself one-handed on a branch and righting herself before she hit the ground. Abe felt the breath catch in his throat. Hope did it every time, and every time it seemed to freeze his heart.

Abe smiled. It seemed to be his fate to be surrounded by incredible women. Even Cyrano had shown her true colors and birthed a little litter of

Skullrons. Abe looked out over the twisted treetops at the brave new world of the Wilds.

Little did Abe know that it would only be a year until his daughter had to face Ol' bear in single combat, but that's a story for another time.

The End

ABOUT THE AUTHOR

C. J. Maloney began his tales of World City as a series of short stories told to his boys at bedtime. These all seemed to come from the same world of World Corp. So he wove them together to tell the story of Finder, a boy who finds his place in the world in Miner Six, and now about Abe and Ellie finding each other.

When he isn't writing, C.J. Maloney helps sick people, takes care of his family, argues with his dog, and tries to thwart the squirrels who get into his bird feeders. His favorite things in life are snuggling and trying to beat his wife at Sudoku, even though he usually loses.

If you enjoyed this book, a range of other books are available at chrisjlmaloney.com.

Please take a moment to make an honest review of this book online. It's the greatest gift you can give another reader and me! Thanks so much!

www.ingramcontent.com/pod-product-compliance
Lightning Source LLC
Chambersburg PA
CBHW052012150726

47999CB00004B/1632